MURPHY'S LAW

Visit us at www.boldstrokesbooks.com

By the Author

In Medias Res

Rum Spring

Lucky Loser

Month of Sundays

Murphy's Law

MURPHY'S LAW

by
Yolanda Wallace

2013

MURPHY'S LAW
© 2013 BY YOLANDA WALLACE. ALL RIGHTS RESERVED.

ISBN 10: 1-60282-773-7
ISBN 13: 978-1-60282-773-8

THIS TRADE PAPERBACK ORIGINAL IS PUBLISHED BY
BOLD STROKES BOOKS, INC.
P.O. BOX 249
VALLEY FALLS, NY 12185

FIRST EDITION: JANUARY 2013

CREDITS
EDITOR: CINDY CRESAP
PRODUCTION DESIGN: SUSAN RAMUNDO
COVER DESIGN BY SHERI (GRAPHICARTIST2020@HOTMAIL.COM)

Acknowledgments

Someone recently asked me why I choose to have such a wide variety of settings in my books instead of deciding to focus on my Savannah hometown. Long story short, my partner and I love to travel. We've been to Mexico, the Bahamas, Italy, Belgium, and the Dominican Republic. In a way, I guess I'm trying to take my readers along for the ride.

The book that follows takes place in the mountains of Nepal. Though the Himalayas are located in a region of the world I have yet to visit, I hope my many hours of research have helped me to bring their jaw-dropping beauty to the printed page.

I remain indebted to Radclyffe and her team at Bold Strokes Books. You make me feel supported, appreciated, and a part of a steadily-growing family. My thanks also go to my editor, Cindy Cresap. With each book, you make me appear to be a much better writer than I actually am. Don't stop!

Thank you, the readers, for continuing to support my work. It's a thrill for me each time I hear that something I've written has resonated with you in some way. Keep the comments coming.

And last but not least, thank you, Dita, for always being there for me whether I'm pecking away at the keyboard or struggling to expand on an idea. In case I haven't told you lately, you're the best.

Dedication

To Dita,
Life is composed of a series of peaks and valleys,
but you help me reach the summit every time.

CHAPTER ONE

I don't like the looks of that sky."

Samantha "Sam" Murphy squinted up at the ominous clouds rolling in over Annapurna. Bad weather was on the way. Maybe not in the next few hours, but definitely in the next few days.

"Neither do I," Rae de Voest said.

Sam and Rae ran The View from the Top Outfitters, a company that offered guided climbs of the world's tallest mountains. Kilimanjaro, Everest, Fuji, and especially the Himalayas. In less than twenty-four hours, Sam was scheduled to lead an expedition up Annapurna I, a section of the Himalayas considered the world's most dangerous peak. The mountain was tough enough on its own. She didn't need Mother Nature to give it a helping hand.

"I thought the monsoon season was over," Rae said.

"Looks like we thought wrong." Sam pulled off her faded Minnesota Twins cap and ran a hand through her hair. "Are you sure you don't want to lead this one?"

"Positive. I'll hold down the fort at base camp while you and our lovely paying clients freeze your buns off on the mountainside."

Sam put her hat back on and tucked her hair behind her ears. "I'll remember that when it's your turn to babysit."

She and Rae took turns acting as head guide, though each readily admitted Sam was better leading the climbs and Rae was better running the day-to-day operations. Sam would rather make an arduous six-week slog through thick snow and thin air than remain at base camp during a climb. She didn't mind poring over topographic charts or watching the radar, but she hated sitting next to the radio with the climb physician waiting to be called on for help while simultaneously hoping the call never came. She would rather anticipate a problem and prevent it than clean up after an issue arose.

"When is Dr. Bradshaw arriving?" she asked.

Rae followed her into the industrial-sized tent that served as their onsite headquarters.

"She and her team landed in Kathmandu a fortnight ago. Jimmy's been leading them on a series of hikes along the Thorong La Pass since then to help them find trust as a team and build up each team member's endurance for the ascent. They've been making steady progress up the mountain."

Sam nodded in approval. The Thorong La Pass topped out at five thousand four hundred meters, well short of Annapurna I's eight thousand meter peak, but hikes along the Pass would help Dr. Bradshaw and her team adjust to the altitude without exhausting them for the ordeal to come.

Rae consulted her battered watch. "If they maintain their current pace, they should be here in about an hour."

Sam hung her fleece jacket on a coat tree and poured herself a large cup of the motor oil Rae called coffee. Then she headed to the conference room so she could take a look at the weather forecast on her laptop.

"Are you considering pushing back the climb?" Rae asked as Sam sat at the conference table and pulled up her favorite meteorological website.

"If we leave too early, we might get wet. If we wait, we might get wet. Either way, we're going to get wet."

Sam debated her options as she examined the picture of the brewing storm on the radar.

"The climb should take between six and eight weeks," she said, thinking out loud. "According to the radar, this system is a slow-mover. It should arrive in two, three days max. If I complete the orientation today and leave bright and early tomorrow morning as scheduled, we'll have a twenty-four hour head start. Plenty of time to complete the first climb and set up camp before the weather sets in. But if the weather system moves faster than anticipated or a member of the team moves slower than expected, the oncoming storm will drench us before we have time to set up our tents." She cocked her head as the wind began to whistle. "I hope everyone brought an extra set of warm, dry clothes. They might need it."

"I'm sure they're prepared. Dr. Bradshaw has been planning this expedition for months. This is supposed to be a fund-raising expedition, not a pleasure cruise. Donors have ponied up hundreds of thousands of dollars to help her charity provide medical care to those who need it most. A successful summit will result in thousands more. The world is watching. The media will be covering every step of the climb from BC to the summit." Rae paused, looking pensive. "As head guide, you'll probably be expected to meet with the press when the climb is over. Are you ready for your close-up?"

At one time, Sam had relished press attention. For more than a decade, however, she had tried to avoid it at all costs. "I'll worry about that when the time comes."

She opened the dossier she had compiled on the members of Dr. Bradshaw's multinational team. All six were experienced climbers. Each had made multiple ascents and four had tackled Everest, the once-mythic mountain that was now practically a tourist attraction based on the amount of foot traffic on its slopes. But none had ever attempted a climb of this magnitude. Sam wasn't surprised. Annapurna I's enormous ice cliffs and imposing seracs, blocks of ice formed by intersecting crevasses on a glacier, were enough to frighten most people away. Most of the ones brave enough to accept the challenge had failed miserably.

Though Annapurna I was only the tenth tallest mountain in the world, ranking between Pakistan's Nanga Parbat and Gasherbrum I on the famed list of fourteen mountains that topped eight thousand meters, it was tops on another list. Its nearly forty percent fatality-to-summit ratio was the worst of all the eight thousanders.

Sam stared at a glossy eight-by-ten photo. She rubbed her thumb across the image of an attractive woman with long, light brown hair and piercing green eyes. She hoped the woman in the picture knew what she was in for. If not, she would soon find out.

She rolled a cigar between her fingers. She wasn't a regular smoker, but she lit up after each successful climb. With the obstacles lining the path of her latest ascent, this Cohiba was going to taste better than all the others. She closed the folder. "This would be so much easier if the good doctor had decided to climb something smaller."

"Preferably European with huts staffed by sexually adventurous twentysomethings."

"Cradle robber."

In Europe, a series of mountain huts dotted the alpine regions. The structures varied in size and craftsmanship—the ones in remote areas were rudimentary at best—though most contained a communal dining room and dormitory-style bedrooms. Guests were encouraged to bring their own sleeping bag liners, but mattresses, blankets, and pillows were provided. In the summer, all the huts were staffed by full-time or volunteer employees. Some even sold bottled water, snacks, and hot meals.

"Would you turn down a gig like that?" Rae asked.

Sam shrugged. "Easy money. Easy living."

Rae leaned back in her seat. "But you're not the kind of woman who likes to do things the easy way. Something tells me the good doctor isn't either."

"This is going to be harder than I thought," Dr. Olivia Bradshaw said as her heart rate began to quicken.

She pressed two fingers against the right side of her neck and looked at her watch. Her pulse was faster than she wanted it to be, but at least it was no longer racing. Chalking up her rapid heartbeat to an adrenaline spike, she looked at the overcast sky. October and November were supposed to be the best months to climb in Nepal—the weather was clear, and freezing temperatures were limited to heights above three thousand meters—but those definitely looked like snow clouds.

"Great. One more thing to worry about. Flight delays, lost luggage, food poisoning. So many things have gone wrong on this trip. I'm ready for something to go right."

She had been training at altitude in her native Colorado for the past six months, but the air in Kathmandu was so thin she had been tempted to ask for an oxygen mask by the time she walked from the tarmac to the terminal at Tribhuvan International Airport. Two weeks later and several thousand feet higher, the boulder had finally rolled off her chest and most of her lightheadedness had disappeared. Just in time, too. Once she and her fellow climbers reached the Annapurna Base Camp, there would be no turning back.

She was ready to get this climb underway. The trip had been her idea. A philanthropic mission, yes, but also a challenge she had laid down for herself because she wanted to see how far she could push her limits. She hadn't anticipated the resulting media circus, but she planned on using it to her advantage. She could raise awareness and her own profile at the same time. Now she had to make sure she didn't blow her opportunity.

She needed to make it up the mountain and down again, preferably in one piece with her entire team intact. To achieve her goal, she needed to do something she rarely did—rely on someone else's expertise instead of her own. There was a reason she had chosen the women from The View from the Top to lead the climb. Sam Murphy, the lead guide, had the best safety record in the business. If she looked as good as her results, she might earn an unexpected bonus at the end of the trip.

"Hey, Doc. Are you ready to do this?" Chance Bennett, the starting point guard for the Denver Nuggets, held out his hand.

"Ready, willing, and able."

She obliged Chance with a fist bump. He responded with the brilliant smile that had earned him a fortune in endorsements aside from his already hefty contract.

"That's what I wanted to hear."

They had been friends since their days as undergraduates at the University of Colorado. Olivia had followed his career in the NBA as closely as he had followed hers in the medical field. They had seen each other through good times and bad. He was there for her whenever she struggled to treat a patient; she was there for him when his team lost a playoff series he thought they should have won. She couldn't think of a better person to have her back as she embarked on the biggest challenge she had ever faced.

She regarded the rest of her team as they continued their trek up Annapurna I's verdant base. Puerto Rican native Beatriz "Gigi" Garcia, the co-chair of the foundation she had established to service the underprivileged at home and abroad. Peter Schneider, the German reporter who would produce daily vlogs to document the excursion. Marie-Eve Dubois, the Canadian women's hockey star who had brought her Olympic gold medal for luck. And last but not least, Hong Kong businessman Roland Chang, who was tagging along to make sure the expedition he had sponsored went according to plan.

Roland looked green around the gills—his stomach had not been able to keep pace with his adventurous palate on their circuitous route around the base of the Annapurna mountain range—but he pronounced himself fit to continue the climb.

Olivia turned to Gigi for a second opinion. The petite surgeon from San Juan took Roland's vitals before giving him the thumbs-up. "Stay away from the yak pot stickers and we'll see you at the top."

"Have you tried them? They're surprisingly good. Especially when you pair them with spinach soup and a glass of millet beer."

Marie-Eve screwed up her face. "I'll stick to energy bars and Moosehead, thanks."

"I'm with you," Peter said, "though I'd prefer a nice German lager to the swill you Canucks call beer."

"The next time I'm in Munich, you'll have to take me for a taste test."

"It's a deal."

The group chatted happily throughout the easy three-hour hike only to fall silent when they neared the Annapurna Conservation Area. Annapurna I, its craggy peak camouflaged by clouds, towered above them. The south face, the side they were supposed to climb, was so steep it almost seemed perpendicular to the ground.

Olivia placed a hand over her racing heart. She had chosen Annapurna I because it was one of the most difficult and dangerous to climb. The massif looked as intimidating as its reputation, but she was excited instead of awed. She had done everything she could to prepare for this challenge. Now it was time to see what she was made of.

"What's the fastest anyone has ever climbed Annapurna I?" she asked the porters' organizer.

He looked at her uneasily. He barely reached Olivia's shoulder, but his strength and endurance were prodigious. She had seen him easily carry loads that would have buckled the knees of even the most bulked-up bodybuilder. "Climbing is not about speed. Going fast gets you in trouble every time. If you want to go fast, take it up with Sam."

He nodded as if he considered the matter closed. Olivia let him have his way. For now.

For her, speed was a way of life. She loved taking risks. Her friends told her she had a death wish. She begged to differ. What she had was a life wish. She wanted to get as much as possible out of hers because it could be over before she knew it.

Most of the chances she had taken had paid off. Taking on Annapurna I was the biggest gamble of them all and she might as well roll the dice.

"Is Jimmy your given name?"

As in the tradition of his people, his last name was Sherpa. She felt certain his first was equally exotic.

"My real name is Gyalchhen."

He told the story of an English tourist who had nicknamed him Jimmy because he reminded her of a lost love from her youth. The pet name had stuck.

"Gyalchhen. Jimmy. Sometimes even my wife doesn't know what to call me. Lucky for her, I answer to both."

He stopped in front of a tent that appeared large enough to house a small circus. Olivia half-expected a troupe of horn-honking clowns to mark their arrival. Instead, two women—a blonde and a brunette—walked out to greet them. The blonde introduced herself first.

"You must be Dr. Bradshaw," she said, sticking out her hand. Her long hair fell well past her shoulders. Laugh lines creased her oval face. "We've spoken on the phone several times, but we've never officially met. Rae de Voest."

"It's a pleasure to finally meet you."

"How was your trip up the mountain?"

Olivia could tell Rae was a charmer. Her strong South African accent added to her appeal.

"Some of the accommodations were interesting, to say the least," Olivia said diplomatically. The first hotel had been pretty good, but a couple had been absolute nightmares. Flea-infested rat holes featuring rooms with wooden platforms for beds and iron stoves that burned dried yak dung instead of firewood. She changed the subject rather than relive the memory. Once was enough. "I couldn't help noticing your accent. I've been meaning to ask you for months now. Are you from Pretoria or Johannesburg?"

"Jo'burg."

"I know it well. I was lucky enough to visit during the World Cup a few years ago."

"I wish the home team could have had a better showing, but I trust you had a pleasant stay in my homeland."

"I did. Thank you for asking. Cold beer. Warm, friendly locals. Who could ask for more?"

"Next time you go, please let me know." Rae's voice dropped an octave into what Olivia assumed was her come-hither register. "I'd be happy to be your tour guide."

"I'll keep that in mind," Olivia said, resorting to diplomacy once more. Rae was sexy but not her type.

She turned to the woman at Rae's side. Her sweat-stained baseball cap was worn low, most likely to guard against the same brisk wind that kept finding its way inside the collar of Olivia's parka. Her short black hair held a smattering of gray, though her wind-burned face was unlined save for the faint crow's feet that framed dark blue eyes that reminded Olivia of a new pair of jeans. She was relatively short—only five-six or five-seven, if that—but she projected confidence, making her seem much taller. Where Rae was beautiful, her companion was handsome. The kind of woman who could easily find her way into Olivia's bed. Olivia introduced herself and waited for a response.

"Samantha Murphy. Call me Sam."

I'd rather call a cab to take us to the nearest hotel.

"Pleased to meet you." Sam didn't look as good as her results. She looked even better. Olivia held her gaze until Chance cleared his throat.

"What are we, chopped liver?"

"I'm sorry." She reluctantly let go of Sam's hand. "Please allow me to introduce the rest of my team."

"I hope you're as excited to be here as we are to have you here," Sam said after all the introductions were made and handshakes were exchanged all around. "If Jimmy has done his job as well as I suspect, he has helped you increase your stamina and your ability to function at altitude. Soon it will be my turn to test both. You'll be seeing a great deal of me over the coming days and weeks. I'll be your guide during the climb. If you'll follow me, I'll show you to your quarters." She led them inside. "The accommodations won't remind you of a five-star hotel, but at least they're warm. Although the temperatures are pretty pleasant right now, they'll drop precipitously when the sun goes down."

Olivia and her team trailed Sam and Rae to a room filled with military-style cots that looked like remnants from World War II. A small bookcase between two of the cots was filled with worn paperback and hardback books recounting famous climbs. Successful and failed attempts to conquer mountains both great and small. Black-and-white pictures of Mt. Everest and Annapurna were taped to the sides of the bookcase. Photographs of famous adventurers were interspersed between them. Robert Peary, the first man to reach the North Pole. Roald Amundsen, the first man to reach the South Pole. Sir Edmund Hillary and Tenzing Norgay, the first men to reach the summit of Mt. Everest. Edurne Pasaban, the first woman to climb the world's fourteen highest peaks.

Olivia was impressed by the display. Climbing purists bemoaned the commercialization of guided expeditions. Olivia understood their complaints. Many of the most famous mountains, Everest especially, had been climbed so many times they had lost some of their allure. But it was obvious Sam and Rae were attracted by the adventure of mountain climbing not the lucre that could be earned as a result.

Olivia and her team wearily dropped their oversized backpacks on the canvas floor and tentatively tested the cots' sturdiness. Chance, the tallest and heaviest at six foot eight and two hundred twenty-five pounds, went first. The cot creaked but remained intact.

"If it'll hold me, you'll be fine." He winked at Gigi, who was eighteen inches shorter and more than one hundred pounds lighter.

Gigi stuck out her tongue. Her baby face made her look as juvenile as her impulsive act.

"We e-mailed you this list before the trip began. In case you didn't bring yours, here's an extra copy."

Sam handed each of them a comprehensive checklist. The spreadsheet was divided into sections delineating everything from clothes to climbing equipment to camping gear. Radio buttons next to each line item indicated what the climbers were expected to provide and what the women from The View from the Top would supply.

"This list encompasses everything you'll need for the expedition. Your supply items are bundled over there." Sam pointed to the far side of the room, where six orderly piles of equipment lay. "Each pile is clearly labeled so you'll be able to tell what belongs to whom. Go through the items and make sure Rae and I got your sizes right. I'm not naming any names, but the handwriting on some of your forms was a bit difficult to read."

Chance elbowed Olivia in the ribs. "I think she means you."

"Speak for yourself. The chicken scratch you call an autograph is worse than mine."

"After you complete your inventory," Sam continued, "meet us in the conference room for an equipment demo and a light lunch. We'll give you a few minutes to relax and sort everything out. See you in thirty."

"What's a crampon?" Chance asked after Sam and Rae left the room. "Is it anything like what my wife sends me to the store for from time to time to keep my ego in check?"

"No," Gigi said, her tanned cheeks tinted pink.

"And from what I've seen," Olivia added, "nothing can keep your ego in check."

"Except for Dirk Nowitzki," Peter said, referring to the Dallas NBA team's star power forward. "The Mavericks had your number last year."

"Oh, you got jokes, huh? We'll see who's laughing when the season starts. Dirk and the Mavs will be in my house on Christmas Day and I don't plan on being a charming host."

Olivia let Chance and Peter go back-and-forth for a few minutes before she put an end to their good-natured bantering. "Okay, guys." She began ticking off items on her checklist. "Let's get the fun stuff done so we can see what our tour guide has to say."

Sam eyed the motley crew systematically decimating the tray of food on the conference table. If they worked as a team, they could accomplish feats they could never achieve individually. But a team was only as strong as its weakest member. If they didn't trust one another, the weak link would soon reveal itself. How many would make it up the mountain? All? Some? Half? Most? Whatever their number, it was her job to make sure they made it back alive.

"What's your assessment?" she asked as she and Jimmy stood in the back of the room.

"They all have good technique and excellent stamina," he replied in Nepali.

She sensed his hesitation. "But?"

"You may need to keep your eye on her." He discreetly indicated Dr. Bradshaw. "On the way here, she kept trying to push the pace instead of following the one I set. Her enthusiasm might cause her to make a mistake she might not be able to recover from."

Sam wasn't surprised to hear a powerful woman like Olivia Bradshaw had trouble ceding control. "She's used to giving orders not taking them."

"I know," Jimmy said with a grin. "She reminds me of you."

He slipped out of the room before she could attempt to defend herself.

"You should hear him describe the looks on their faces the first time they saw the mountain," Rae whispered. "He said it was like they'd simultaneously shit their shorts."

Sam snorted laughter. She had experienced a reaction identical to theirs the first time she stood at the base of Mt. Everest. "Priceless."

"I'll bet you a thousand rupees at least one of them won't even begin the attempt tomorrow."

Sam performed a quick calculation. Based on the current exchange rates, a thousand rupees was around twenty American dollars. With the money they were making from this trip, she could afford to take a risk.

"My money's on Chance," Rae said. "Is he really going to put himself through the torture of a climb this strenuous so close to the start of a season most think will be his last?"

"From what I could gather, he appears to be Dr. Bradshaw's best friend. He's come this far. There's no way he's going to let her down now. I think Mr. Moneybags over there will be the one who backs out." She glanced at Roland Chang, who was halfway through his third club sandwich. "He's in this for the adventure. After I complete my spiel, he's going to realize he's already had all the adventure he can take."

Rae held out her hand, pinky extended. "I'll take that bet."

Sam curled her pinky around Rae's, then strode to the front of the room and addressed her audience. "Let's get started." She faltered when she saw Dr. Bradshaw gazing at her intently. She had given the preparedness speech a thousand times, but one look from this woman had her so flustered she couldn't remember a word. Women never got under her skin. In her pants, yes, but this was something different. What was it about Dr. Bradshaw that had her so on edge? She cleared her throat, giving herself an extra moment to gather her thoughts.

"The good news is you've already made it past the four thousand meter mark. The bad news is you have another four thousand meters to go. Give yourselves a hand for being halfway through your first eight thousander. That's quite an accomplishment." She led the room in a round of applause, taking note of the group's obvious camaraderie as they whistled, cheered, and slapped one another on the back. She hoped their high spirits wouldn't begin to flag as the air grew thinner and tempers grew shorter.

"Thank you for choosing Rae, myself, Jimmy, and the rest of our team to lead you on your climb. We're going to do everything possible to help you complete your mission. If you start to suffer from information overload, please let me know and I'll give you a few minutes to decompress. We have a lot to go over, so let's get started. The first part of today's session might bore you to tears, but bear with me. The information I'm about to impart could save your lives in the days and weeks to come."

She smiled to herself when each member of the quintet perked up. The line never failed to get everyone's attention. Now that she had it, she couldn't let it go to waste.

She listed each piece of equipment and demonstrated its use. Everything from the carabiners to the climbing harnesses to the ice axes. Even the foam earplugs designed to block out the noise of the tent material flapping from the wind threatening to rip the temporary shelter from its moorings and send the sleeping climbers sliding down the mountain.

"The Himalayas are a place of spiritual refuge for many people and must be treated with respect. I like to use small teams in order to limit damage to the mountain, so we'll use a ratio of one porter to two climbers. Jimmy, Tenzing, Lhakpa, and Mingma are here to assist you, but they aren't your personal butlers. It's up to you to make sure you follow the Leave No Trace guidelines and reduce your impact on the environment. If any of you are high maintenance, please let me know now and I'll arrange transport to the nearest hotel with concierge service."

No one took her up on her offer.

"Pasang, who provided your lunch today, will be traveling with us to make sure we don't go hungry. Because if you have to depend on me to do the cooking, we might starve before the first week is up."

She pointed to the smiling teenager who was refilling everyone's water glasses. He was Jimmy's younger son. Unlike his brother Dinesh the monk, he wanted to follow in his father's footsteps. Sam had given him an entry-level position as cook while he worked on his climbing skills. If he was anything like his father, he would move up from cook to climber in no time—resulting in a bump in pay and earning him rock star status in his village. Here in Nepal, climbers were revered almost as much as the mountains themselves.

"We'll want to be as light as possible so Jimmy and his crew will carry most of the equipment and supplies until it's time to use them. Non-perishable items will be rationed between each camp during the ascent. The camps will remain in place until we descend, at which time we'll break camp and erase all signs we were ever there. I can't stress this enough. Leave No Trace means just that. Everything we take with us has to come back with us. And I mean everything. Police your areas at night. I don't want to see any discarded cigarette butts or empty soda cans. If I do, it's a fifty dollar fine per infraction, which is a hell of a lot cheaper than the penalty imposed by the Nepalese government."

Sam felt like a headmistress admonishing the incoming class on the first day of school. She hoped her charges were paying attention.

"Now that you're sufficiently chastened, let's move on to one of the most important items in our arsenal." She patted a portable oxygen tank. "After we reach the seven thousand meter mark, which is approximately twenty-three thousand feet, you'll want to use the oxygen." She showed how to affix the mask and turn on the gas. She waited for each member of the team to follow her lead before she continued. "A handful of expert climbers have managed to reach the summit without using supplemental oxygen. Sherpas do it on a routine basis. A few of you might want to try to duplicate their feat. You're free to try, but I wouldn't recommend it. You'll want to have your wits about you at all times. To do that, you'll need to have a clear head. Once we pass fifteen thousand feet, even the simplest tasks will seem like quantum physics."

She put away her props. "Now for the outerwear. The weather here is pretty mild this time of year. Sixties during the day, forties to fifties at night. Fahrenheit, that is. Even after all these years, my Celsius conversion is still a little shaky. Shorts and a light jacket should be okay for the first couple of legs, but make sure you pack rain gear and cold weather attire for the subsequent segments."

"What about snow?" Marie-Eve asked. "I expected it to be freezing, but it's warmer here than it is at home. I'm beginning to think I brought my skates for nothing."

Sam laughed quietly, remembering an interview Marie-Eve gave in her hometown newspaper in which she said she planned to climb up the mountain but skate down it. Ten years ago, Sam might have said something along those lines, but the amount of her bravado decreased as the number of candles on her birthday cake increased. Was she really about to turn thirty-seven? It seemed like just yesterday she was twenty-five. But that was two lifetimes, dozens of climbs, and several thousand miles ago.

"Like the old saying goes, if you don't like the weather, wait fifteen minutes; it'll change. Nepal has four seasons: winter, spring, monsoon, and autumn. The monsoon season ended last month. Most of the lower elevations shouldn't see snow until late November or early December, but don't be surprised if we see a few flakes before we reach the top."

"Are those rain clouds or snow clouds I see coming down the mountain?" Dr. Bradshaw asked. "According to my research, some October trekkers have run into torrential rains, golf ball-sized hail, and freak snowstorms. I'd like to know what you think we're in for."

Sam, who had been in complete control once she began her presentation, felt herself getting lost in those green eyes. "Um, those are, uh—"

"Rain clouds," Rae cut in. "If you're worried about blizzards and whiteouts, don't be. We shouldn't see real weather for a couple of months. My advice is something you as a physician have likely said more than once: prepare for the worst and expect the best."

Sam quickly regained her footing. "Nepal's unspoiled beauty makes it a popular destination for nature lovers. While Jimmy led you here, I'm sure you noticed the crowds of trekkers on the paths." Dr. Bradshaw and her team murmured in agreement. "Pretty soon, those crowds will disappear and we'll pretty much have the mountain to ourselves. Two other teams will be making ascents this month, but both will be at least a week behind us."

She flipped on the overhead projector. A colorful map of Annapurna I appeared on the wall. "This is the route I intend for us to take." She directed the beam of her laser pointer at the map. "As you can tell from these markers, we'll set up camp at various elevations. Six 'permanent' camps and several temporary ones. If everything goes according to plan, we'll reach Camp Two by the end of the first week, Camp Four by the middle of the third week, and Camp Six by the beginning of the fifth. Then we'll return to base camp for a few days to marshal our strength before we begin our assault on the summit. The last temporary camp will be placed here at the base of the ice wall." She indicated a spot on the map that represented an area over twenty-two thousand feet up. "Once we clear the ice wall, we'll move to the most difficult part of the climb—the rock bands at twenty-four thousand and twenty-five thousand feet. Make it past those and it's clear sailing to the summit."

"If it isn't proprietary, I'd like a copy of your map," Dr. Bradshaw said. "I want to bump it up against some of the topographic charts I downloaded in Kathmandu to check for anomalies. I'd also like a copy of the latest Doppler readout to see just how large the approaching storm is."

Sam admired her attention to detail. Was she always this thorough—and this sexy? "I reconnoitered the mountain last month and didn't see any changes from previous trips, but I'd be more than happy to provide you with any information you feel you may need. As a matter of fact, we'll make copies for each of you." She pulled the slide off the projector and handed it to Rae.

"I'm on it," Rae said. "Back in a tick."

"Now that we've run through the basics," Sam said after Rae left to prepare the requested documentation, "let's move on to survival techniques. The most difficult factors to consider when mountaineering are weather conditions, which can be predicted, and avalanches, which cannot. As Dr. Bradshaw pointed out, we have a weather system rolling in. It might dump a couple of inches of rain on us and muddy the track a bit, but—fingers crossed—I don't expect it to be a cause of concern."

She paused before moving to the unpleasant part of her speech. "Annapurna is Sanskrit for 'full of food.' Don't take that literally. This mountain is never full; it's always hungry. Avalanches are how she eats. In case we're unlucky enough to be swept up in one, we'll each be supplied with an inflatable air bag that we'll keep in our backpacks and an avalanche beacon that we'll keep on us at all times." She held up the beacon, a small battery-powered radio transceiver that fit in the palm of her hand. "The beacon sends a signal alerting rescuers to your position if you're buried under the snow. The signal broadcasts for hours. After fifteen minutes, though, the mission could change from search and rescue to retrieval."

She watched the import of her words sink in.

"But there are techniques you can employ to be proactive. First of all, get the fuck out of the way. Move to the side, try to jump upslope past the fracture line, swim to stay near the surface, dance a jig if you want. Just don't stand there mesmerized. If you do, you'll be carried downhill. Second, if you can't escape, grab on to something solid like a boulder or a tree. Third, if you know you're going to be buried, create an air pocket. When the avalanche slows down but before the snow settles, cup your hands in front of your mouth. The resulting air pocket should provide enough air to last for half an hour, plenty of time for someone to find you and dig you out. Just before the snow settles, take a deep breath and hold it for a few seconds. This will give you the breathing room you'll need once the snow hardens around you. Finally, conserve your air and your energy. Try to free yourself after the snow settles, but don't jeopardize your air pocket in order to do it. If you're close to the surface, dig yourself out. But if not, don't waste your breath. Remain calm and wait for help to arrive. Any questions so far?"

"I have one." The reporter raised his hand. With his spiky blond hair and wispy facial hair, he bore more than a passing resemblance to Big Bird. Sam doubted he would appreciate the comparison so she kept the observation to herself. "I admit this is a rather morbid question, but I have to ask. Nearly sixty people have died trying to climb this mountain. During your years as a guide, how many climbers have you lost?"

Sam could feel the tension ratchet up another notch. She had to put everyone at ease while making sure they didn't completely let down their guard.

"Have you heard of Murphy's Law?"

Peter tapped his pen on the table like a star student who wasn't being sufficiently challenged in class. "Anything that can go wrong will go wrong."

"My version is a little different. For the next six weeks, Murphy's Law says this: no one dies on my watch."

CHAPTER TWO

Olivia tossed the thin sheet and scratchy wool blanket off her restless body, swung her legs over the side of the cot, and pushed herself to her feet. She couldn't sleep, and she refused to be serenaded by the snores of five people who didn't share her affliction.

She pulled a bright orange Denver Broncos sweatshirt over her long-sleeved silk undershirt and reached under her cot for her battery-powered LED headlamp. She secured the elastic strap and turned on the light so she could find her way to the bookcase. She picked out a book, not bothering to check the title or subject matter. She tucked the book under her arm, picked up her hiking boots, and tiptoed out of the room. Near the exit, she stepped into her shoes but didn't lace them up. She didn't plan on venturing far. She simply needed a change of scenery to keep the proverbial walls from closing in.

She opened the tent flap and stepped out into the inky blackness. The weather felt as mild as a Colorado fall—until the gusting wind reminded her she was a long, long way from home.

She shoved her hands in the pockets of her gray sweatpants. She tried to locate Annapurna I's distant peak, but clouds covered the moon, limiting her field of visibility to a few feet. An animal howled in the darkness. A wolf?

"No way. Not at this elevation." She laughed nervously. "Maybe the mythical Abominable Snowman isn't so mythical after all."

She sat on an upturned sal tree stump. The surface, rubbed smooth by frequent use, was so shiny it seemed shellacked. She directed the light beam at the book she had randomly selected. Maurice Herzog's classic tale of his expedition's harrowing experiences on Annapurna I.

She started in surprise at the distinctive sound of a bottle being opened. The click of the cap being twisted followed by the hiss of escaping carbonated air.

"Who's there?"

"Relax. It's only me." Sam, the handsome tour guide, appeared so suddenly she seemed to have materialized out of thin air. She shielded her eyes from the glare of the beam from the headlamp. Olivia switched off the light. Sam offered her a bottle of beer. Olivia didn't recognize the label. "Gorkha. It's not Bud Light, but it'll do in a pinch."

"Under normal circumstances, I'd take you up on your offer but I'm abstaining from alcohol until the climb's over. I haven't had anything stronger than protein shakes since March."

"You're a better woman than I am." Sam wrapped her lips around the bottle's opening and took a long pull.

Olivia felt her mouth water. And not for the beer. She mended broken bodies for a living. She didn't have time to treat broken hearts as well. One-night stands and friends with benefits were more her style. So was Sam Murphy.

The clouds overhead had parted, allowing the moon's bright light to shine through. Sam tilted the book in Olivia's hands, pointing it toward the moon so she could see the title. "Not the subject matter I would have chosen the night before attempting to climb the same mountain, but to each her own."

Olivia shivered as Sam's fingers brushed against hers, the calloused tips sliding across the back of her hand. The rush of adrenaline felt like a chill. She crossed her arms as the wind picked up again. "I saw you this afternoon."

"Was I doing something I shouldn't?"

"You were doing your homework."

After that afternoon's readiness meeting/training session, while everyone else was resting or taking pictures for posterity, Sam had spent hours studying charts and maps in the ready room.

"I was tempted to join you, but I didn't want to intrude."

Sam shrugged. "You wouldn't have been intruding."

"That's not what it felt like to me."

"What did it feel like to you?"

Olivia narrowed her eyes. Damn, this woman was hard to read. Did she want her to move closer or go away? "You strike me as a woman who enjoys her privacy."

"I enjoy being private. There's a difference."

Olivia wished she hadn't turned down that beer. Serious thought required alcohol. "And the difference is?"

"One means I prefer being left alone; the other means my business is my own."

"So I shouldn't ask you how it feels to be one of the handful of women who have climbed the seven summits?"

The highest mountains on each of the seven continents were Kilimanjaro, Vinson Massif, Everest, Kosciusko, Elbrus, McKinley, and Acongua in Africa, Antarctica, Asia, Australia, Europe, North America, and South America respectively. Few climbers could claim to have reached the summit of all seven. Sam Murphy was one of the few.

"I see you've done your homework as well. I don't know how to answer your question without seeming like a pompous ass, so I'll simply say it feels pretty good. Not as good as it would feel to have climbed all fourteen eight thousanders, but give me a call after I conquer Shishapangma and I'll let you know for sure."

Olivia closed her book. The subject at hand was much more interesting than the one on the printed page. "How did you get into climbing?"

"I bristle at authority. Climbing lets me be the one giving orders instead of the one taking them." Sam shifted her weight from one foot to the other as if she wished she hadn't made such a personal admission. She quickly turned the spotlight away from herself and toward Olivia. "How did you become a doctor?"

"Lots of practice. No pun intended."

"None taken."

Sam took another pull of her beer. She reminded Olivia of a cowboy in a vintage Western sizing up the opposition over a drink in the town bar. Where were the stoic sheriff, the comical drunk, and the hooker with a heart of gold?

"Tell me how a girl from the Land of a Thousand Lakes ended up in Nepal."

Sam seemed surprised. "How did you know I was from Minnesota? The seven summits stuff is on our website for all the world to see, but I made sure the webmaster didn't include any personal information."

Olivia pointed to Sam's Twins cap. "Educated guess. I took you for a hometown girl, not an idle fan."

Sam adjusted her hat as her panicked expression gradually faded. "I wear this thing so often I sometimes forget it's there."

"Which part of Minnesota are you from? If that's too personal, you don't—"

"I'm from St. Paul," Sam said the words in a rush as if she were afraid she might decide not to respond if she didn't answer the question quickly—or if she were spitting out the name of the first city that came to mind.

"Relocating must have been quite an adjustment."

"Not really. Minnesota winters are legendarily bad. A friend of mine once poured herself a cup of coffee to drink while she drove to work. The coffee froze solid by the time she walked the twenty feet from her house to her car. Didn't stop her, though. She stuck a tongue depressor in it and licked it like a Popsicle."

Olivia laughed but quickly quieted to avoid disturbing the others. "I have the distinct impression my leg is being pulled."

"Gently, I hope."

I hope that's the first and last time you're gentle with me. She tried to shake the pleasant thought out of her head.

"I understand why you stay, but how did you get here in the first place?"

Sam shrugged. "Rae made me an offer I couldn't refuse."

She waited in vain for Sam to expand on her answer. "How did you two meet?"

"At a rock climbing competition in Italy. When I won, she came along with the prize."

Olivia felt a pang of disappointment. "How long have you been together?"

"Ten years. But we're not *together* together. We're business partners not lovers."

"Oh." She tried to temper her excitement. "I mean, that's cool you can do something you love with someone you...care about."

Sam's lips quirked into a smile. "Some days I'm not so sure. Rae and I are as close as sisters, which means we fight like them, too. But at the end of the day, there's no one I'd rather be in a partnership with."

"I feel the same way about Gigi. Considering we spend more time with each other than we do our families, that's a definite plus."

Sam pawed at the grass with the toe of one boot. "I could tell how close you are by watching you interact during orientation this afternoon. Were the two of you ever an item?"

"Unfortunately, no. She has always had eyes for Chance and he has always had eyes for her. They started dating during freshman year in Boulder and they've been married since the day Chance declared for the draft as a junior. I've never been anything more than a fifth wheel."

"Gigi may be out of the picture, but there's no one at home anxiously awaiting your return? There's no one here waiting for you to come back down the mountain?"

Olivia smiled. Some sack time with Sam could be the perfect remedy for her insomnia. Perhaps her interest was mutual. "If you're asking me if I'm single, yes, I am."

"I wasn't asking."

"Then maybe I'm volunteering the information."

Sam stiffened. "Thanks for the offer, but I don't sleep with clients."

"Understandable. Disappointing, but understandable." Her eyes roamed Sam's body. Sam's black pullover was loose fitting, but her jeans were tight, clinging to thickly muscled legs. Olivia wondered how it would feel to have those strong limbs wrapped around her, squeezing her as she came. "I have a similar rule about sleeping with patients. But you look perfectly healthy to me."

"I should go."

"Don't." She put her hand on Sam's leg but immediately withdrew when Sam backed away as if she had an infectious disease. "I think that's my cue to leave." She stood and turned to make what she hoped would be a graceful exit.

"Dr. Bradshaw—"

"Look. No harm, no foul. I'm a big girl. I know how to take no for an answer. If I came on too strong, I apologize. I assure you it won't happen again. And by the way, it's Olivia. Not even my patients call me Dr. Bradshaw. See you in the morning."

She climbed back in bed with her tail between her legs. She would have preferred to have something else there.

❖

Sam sighed in frustration as she watched Olivia walk away.

"I couldn't have handled that better if I tried."

She sat on the sal stump Olivia had vacated during her abrupt departure and rolled the bottle of Gorkha between her palms.

She wasn't used to answering questions about her personal life. Her professional one, either. Olivia challenged her edicts against both. She had felt so comfortable talking to her—until the conversation turned sexual. She wasn't a prude. Far from it. Why, then, had she reacted so badly when Olivia made it clear she wanted to sleep with her? In fact, the idea of having sex with the gorgeous doctor was pretty damn appealing. But her usual wham, bam, thank-you-ma'am wouldn't do. Not this time. She wanted to get to know Olivia. She wanted Olivia to get to know her. But the thought of sharing her deepest, darkest secrets scared her to death.

Oxygen deprivation on the mountain kept conversation to a minimum during the latter stages of a climb. Aside from the presentation she gave the day before each ascent began, she let Rae do most of the talking. The arrangement worked for all involved. Rae loved to talk and clients loved trying to guess if her accent was English, South African, or Australian. Then Olivia Bradshaw came along and threw a monkey wrench in the well-oiled machine that powered her defensive shields.

They'd just met and Sam already wanted to tell her everything. The story behind the secrets, half-truths, and non-answers. She wanted to talk to her until her voice gave out. Kiss her until her lips went numb. When was the last time she felt that way about someone? Hell, when was the last time she felt anything at all?

Easy. Before Mont Blanc. Before it had taken ten seconds to lose what she had waited twenty-two years to find.

She drained the rest of the beer and reached for another. She needed something stronger. Bourbon, tequila, or a jar of her grandfather's homemade moonshine. She needed to dull her senses. If time healed all wounds, why weren't twelve years long enough to ease the pain?

She finished her beer, placed both bottles in the recycling bin, and returned to the room she and Rae shared when they had clients onsite.

"Is it time?" Rae asked drowsily.

"Almost."

"Where were you?"

"Talking with Dr. Bradshaw."

Rae stifled a yawn. "Lucky you. She's a hell of a lot sexier in person than she is in print. That Marie-Eve is a looker, too. Almost makes me wish I was leading the climb instead of you."

"It's not too late, you know."

"Nah, I'll let you do all the dirty work. Take them to the summit and get their juices flowing. I'll help them celebrate their amazing feat when you return them to BC safe and sound. It's been years since I had a good ménage à trois. Hell, times are tough. I'll even take a bad one at this point."

Sam flinched from a pang of what felt like jealousy. She envied Rae's ability to live life carefree, unburdened by guilt or regret. Why couldn't she do that? She turned and faced the wall. "Sweet dreams, Rae."

Rae yawned again. "Trust me. If my dreams are about Olivia Bradshaw, they'll be as sweet as sugar."

Sam's dreams weren't the kind she cared to remember. They were nightmares best forgotten as soon as the sun rose. She closed her eyes and tried to grab a few hours of sleep before the alarm went off. Tomorrow she could put everything behind her and do what she did best: climb.

CHAPTER THREE

Olivia could feel Sam's eyes on her when she approached the breakfast table. For the next six to eight weeks, they would need to rely on each other. Trust each other implicitly. If they didn't get past the awkward ending to their last encounter, trusting each other would be virtually impossible. She pulled out a cold metal chair and took a seat. "Good morning, everyone," she said, trying to infuse her voice with as much good cheer as she could muster.

Sam didn't respond, but her body language changed from guarded to semi-relaxed. Mission accomplished.

"*Namaste,*" Rae said chirpily. "Did you sleep well?"

"Like a baby." Olivia poured herself a cup of coffee. In truth, she hadn't slept a wink after she returned to bed a few hours ago. She hoped the bags under her eyes wouldn't give her away. She couldn't stop thinking about the climb. A journey of a thousand miles began with a single step and she was about to take the first one. She piled her plate high with scrambled eggs, roasted potatoes, and fresh fruit. Then she poured ketchup on the potatoes and took a bite of the rubbery eggs. "How's the weather? Are we good to go or are we on hold?"

Rae spread butter on a thick slice of bread. "We can push off as soon as Jimmy finishes fueling the portable generator."

"That's great news." She needed to get going. She needed to get her body in motion. She needed to forget. Forget how it felt to have Sam's eyes gazing into hers. Forget how much she wanted to feel Sam's climb-roughened hands sliding over her bare skin. Forget her budding attraction to Sam Murphy even as she followed her twenty-six thousand feet into the sky.

Chance's groans snapped her out of her reverie. His stomach gurgled as if a creature from a bad horror film had set up residence in his intestines. Olivia glanced at his half-empty plate. Known for his enormous appetite, he normally consumed up to five thousand calories a day. Leaving a meal unfinished was unlike him.

"Are you feeling okay?"

Beads of sweat the size of dimes had formed on his shaved head. His clammy skin bore an unhealthy pallor. "I must have caught some kind of bug on the pass. I've been in the crapper all morning. Now I feel like I'm going to puke."

Marie-Eve pushed her plate away from her. "Thanks for over sharing."

Gigi placed a hand on his forehead. "You have a fever, *Papi.*" She dipped her napkin into her glass of water and brushed the damp cloth over his face. "Do you need to stay behind? Why don't you get some rest and catch up to us tomorrow? I'll stay with you if you like."

"Not a chance. If we stay behind, we'll fall behind. Sam has a schedule and I'm sticking to it." He kissed Gigi's palm before reaching for a liter of bottled water. "I'll be fine as soon as I hydrate, though a little TLC from the sexiest doctor in the world wouldn't hurt."

Gigi leaned her head against his shoulder. "I brought medications to treat nausea and diarrhea. They're in my bag if you want me to—"

"Stop worrying so much. I'll give you the high sign if I need anything." He nuzzled her short dark curls.

Olivia checked in on the other members of the team. Peter and Marie-Eve were in the middle of yet another spirited comparison between Canadian and German beer so she left them to it. She turned to Roland, who was on the latest leg of his gastronomic tour of Nepal. She decided to give him the benefit of the doubt. Perhaps he was trying to take in as many calories as he could now so he'd have extra reserves to tap into on the mountain.

"Are you feeling better today?"

"Much better, thank you," Roland said. He licked mulberry jam off his lips and reached for a glass of jackfruit juice. Ripened jackfruit emitted an odor similar to rotting onions. Olivia didn't want to know if the fruit's taste matched its unpleasant smell. "But yesterday's talk of monsoons and blizzards has me thinking. Perhaps it would be best if I remained here at camp until you return. If a healthy young man like Mr. Bennett has taken ill so early in our journey, imagine how much someone like me would slow the team down later on. You have—how do you say in America—no hard feelings?"

"Of course not."

Rae and Sam charged sixty thousand dollars a head to lead clients up Annapurna I. The fee for Everest, a two-month trip, was even higher. The pricing was steep, but thanks to their unblemished record, they had compiled a lengthy list of satisfied customers. Roland had ponied up nearly half a million dollars to fund this trip. Why argue with the man who was paying the bills? If he wanted to watch the action from the bleachers instead of joining in the game, she wouldn't try to cajole him into changing his mind.

He grinned like a naughty boy who had managed to talk his way out of an expected punishment. "I will keep Ms. de Voest and the climb physician company while we anxiously await news of your tremendous achievement."

Olivia had never understood why most climb physicians remained at base camp instead of embarking on the expedition with the people in their care. No matter. She and Gigi could treat the minor maladies that sprang up. If anything more serious arose, help was just a radio call away.

Sam grabbed a piece of toast and clenched it between her teeth while she slipped her arms into the sleeves of her hooded windbreaker. "I'll tell Jimmy we won't need to take as many supplies or as many porters as we originally thought."

Olivia grabbed her rain slicker and followed her outside.

"Anxious to get underway?" Sam tossed her a helmet. The sturdy head covering wasn't decorative. It was meant to protect the wearer from falling rocks, an unfortunate phenomenon that had claimed more than its fair share of climbers. "We're almost ready." She keyed the microphone of a two-way radio.

The small unit featured voice activation, a hand crank to supplement the direct and alternate power supplies, hands-free operation, and a USB port to charge cell phones and mp3 players. If it could drive a stick shift, Olivia might have to marry it.

Sam picked up the handset and held the speaker close to her mouth, her hand cupped over the microphone to block the background noise. "Test one, two, three. Test one, two, three. Rae, do you read me? Over."

The radio crackled and went silent. Sam switched frequencies and repeated her message. A few seconds later, Rae's voice said, "Reading you loud and clear. Over."

"Dr. Bradshaw—"

Olivia laid a hand on Sam's forearm. The corded muscles felt like banded steel. "It's Olivia, remember?"

Sam's dark blue eyes flicked down to Olivia's hand then up to her face. She nodded to acknowledge the correction.

Mindful of Sam's apparent aversion to being touched, Olivia removed her hand before Sam could shake it off.

"*Olivia* is here with me and the guys. Give everyone else five minutes to shit, shower, and shave, then send them out. I'll check in during the rest stop, then again when we set up camp for the night. Over."

"Roger. Keep your head down up there. Over."

"We're only going a couple thousand feet today. Over."

"You know better than anyone there's no *only* on this mountain. Be careful, Sam. Over."

"You got it. As for the thousand rupees you owe me, pay me in cash. I don't take checks. Over."

"Yeah, yeah, yeah. I'll see you when you get back. Over and out."

Olivia secured her helmet and checked the straps on her backpack while Sam supervised the offloading of the extraneous equipment and supplies. The other members of the team slowly came out to join them. Marie-Eve and Peter were first on the scene, followed by Gigi and Chance.

"The gang's all here," Chance said. "Let's get a move on."

One of the Sherpas turned to another of his fellow porters, clearly perplexed by the tall, brown-skinned man handing out high fives. His companion smiled, pointed at Chance, and said something in his native language that sounded remarkably like "Michael Jordan." Olivia chose to keep that bit of misinformation to herself. Chance was a talented player, but his career stats were nowhere near those of the man widely considered to be the best player who ever dribbled a basketball.

Sam held up a cautionary hand. "One more thing before we go."

Marie-Eve groaned. "Not another speech."

Sam leaned casually on her trekking poles as if she had all the time in the world. Olivia could hear the clock ticking. Why couldn't she?

"I know you're all anxious to get started. Please try to keep in mind we aren't going to reach the top in one day. If everything goes according to plan, it will take a little more than five weeks to get to the summit and two to three days to get down. We're going to take the 'climb high, sleep low' approach to give our bodies adequate time to acclimatize to the thinner air. We will climb as high as we can each day, but we won't sleep more than a thousand feet higher than we did the day before."

"It sounds like we're going to be doing the same two steps forward and one step back dance we did on the way up Everest," Chance said for Olivia's benefit.

"If we don't, the virus you're fighting will pale in comparison to the altitude sickness you'll have." Sam's voice hardened, letting everyone know her authority and expertise were not to be questioned. "This is a marathon, not a sprint. Save as much strength as possible. You're going to need every ounce. Today is the easiest leg you're going to have. Remember that in the morning when the temptation to remain inside your nice, warm sleeping bags will be greater than your desire to subject yourself to more punishment."

Sam looked almost gleeful as she made the pronouncement. Olivia shook her head in amusement. Mountain climbers were cut from a different cloth.

Must be the thin air.

❖

Sam stopped to look back at the climbers. Chance, despite his assertions to the contrary during breakfast, was far from okay. Even though they were moving at a snail's pace, he was struggling mightily, lagging a good twenty feet behind the rest of the pack. If he continued to struggle, she'd have to break out the guide ropes a week early. The one hundred fifty foot tethers bound pairs of climbers to each other, allowing the stronger member of the team to help the weaker one. When the time came, she'd assign Jimmy to Chance. Dr. Bradshaw—Olivia—would be her responsibility. Tenzing could pair with Gigi, Lhakpa with Marie-Eve, and Pasang with Peter. But first things first. If Chance's performance didn't improve, not even guide ropes would get him to the summit.

She had expected the altitude to have the least effect on him. He was a professional athlete and a Colorado native, after all. His lung capacity should be higher than the average person's. She would have figured chain-smoking Peter to be the weak link. After the first thousand feet, however, Peter looked as fresh as a daisy and Chance was gasping for breath.

"Are you sure about today being easy?" he asked during the rest break. He unzipped his jacket to get more air. "I guess this damn virus I caught took more out of me than I thought."

Sam looked him over. His face was ashen, his breathing labored. "Tomorrow, we're going to have rougher terrain and ankle-deep mud brought on by precipitation from the storm clouds gathering overhead. Are you fit to continue?" She wasn't a doctor, but in her layman's opinion, the answer was no.

He nodded resolutely. "I've had harder workouts in training camp. When I tell my grandkids about this trip, I don't want to start out by saying Grandpa was a quitter."

"We have to have kids before we can have grandkids, *Papi*," Gigi said.

"Maybe we can work on that after we set up camp tonight. Fair warning, everybody. If the tent's rocking, don't bother knocking."

Sam thought Chance's joke was a lame attempt to deflect attention, but Gigi laughed loyally. "Looks like you're feeling better already."

Sam counted heads. "One, two, three, four, five." *Wait. There should be six.* She felt a momentary surge of panic before she remembered Roland dropped out before they left base camp. Was Chance about to join him? Giving herself a bit of privacy, she walked a few feet away from the group before she radioed Rae. "Is our guest keeping you and Dr. Curtis entertained?"

"He's eating us out of house and home is what he's doing. It's a good thing the supply truck's coming by tomorrow or he might make a meal out of me."

"He wouldn't be the first."

"Not that kind of meal. How's the view up there?"

"Beautiful as always, but I might have to return half the money from our bet."

"What do you mean?"

"I think I have someone coming down with HAPE."

"Already?" Rae's jocularity disappeared as she quickly turned serious.

"HAPE kicks in at twenty-five hundred meters. We're already well past that. At this point, anyone is susceptible."

High Altitude Pulmonary Edema was a malady that affected certain climbers regardless of age, health, or physical conditioning. No one knew what made some people more likely to be stricken with the condition than others, but if left untreated, the resulting fluid accumulation in the lungs could prove fatal.

Dr. Curtis' voice came on the radio. "You're fortunate to have two physicians on the trail with you. Have you consulted with either of them?"

"Not yet. Neither can be counted on to be objective about this particular patient."

She backed off, wanting to be wrong. Chance's presence had added to the media attention the climb had received. If he dropped out, the attention would increase exponentially as every news outlet ran the story. Would Chance's absence hinder Olivia's fund-raising efforts or aid them? Would the increased media attention result in unwanted inquiries into her past? She had way too many questions and not nearly enough answers.

"I could be overreacting," she said. "Perhaps he's simply coming down with a cold."

"Perhaps, but perhaps not. We can't take that chance. How many symptoms of HAPE does the client have?"

Sam watched Chance struggle to catch his breath. "Three so far. His exercise performance is piss poor, he's having difficulty breathing even when he isn't exerting himself, and he's starting to develop a cough. That's in addition to the nausea and diarrhea he mentioned this morning."

Dr. Curtis grunted noncommittally. "That's a tough call. It could be a cold, the remnants of the virus he contracted last night, or a combination of the two. You'd better get Dr. Bradshaw involved. As team leader, she deserves to know what's going on with each member of her party. She can take a look at him and let me know if she thinks he should abandon the expedition. If so, I'll arrange transport to the hospital in Kathmandu for further evaluation."

"You're right. Best friend or not, I think she'll put his well-being ahead of his hubris."

"Keep me posted," Rae said, assuming control of the radio again. "No matter what happens."

"Will do. Over and out."

Almost as if she sensed something was wrong, Olivia joined her as soon as she placed the handset in its cradle. "What's going on?"

Sam whispered her concerns. "I hate to be an alarmist, but I need you to check Chance's oxygen levels. If they're less than ninety percent, we'll need to—"

A line of concern creased Olivia's brow. "You think he's coming down with HAPE." Sam could tell she was harboring the same suspicions.

"It's a possibility."

"He'll want to stay regardless of my diagnosis. As a physician—as his friend—I can't allow him to put his life in danger." Olivia laughed sarcastically, then spread her arms, indicating their surroundings. "Some would say I already have." She dug her medical bag out of her backpack and approached the group resting in an outcropping of large rocks.

"What's that for?" Chance asked defensively.

"I'd like to check you out."

He held out his hands as if to fend her off. "No need, Liv. I'm good."

"Humor me, okay?" She put the diaphragm of her stethoscope on his chest while everyone else gathered around them. So much for doctor-patient confidentiality. "Deep breath in."

She closed her eyes as if to block out everything except what was most important—her patient. "Let it out slow. Good." She moved the diaphragm from the right side of his chest to the left and repeated the process. Then from the front to the back. "No crackles or wheezing and your heart rate's good."

"I told you."

"Before you get too excited, let me check one more thing." She pulled a small device out of her bag and clamped it on his index finger.

"What's this?" he asked.

"A pulse oximeter," Gigi said, obviously concerned. "She's testing the amount of oxygen in your blood." She leaned forward when the device beeped. "What does it say?"

Olivia peered at the readout. "Ninety-two."

Chance looked from Olivia to Gigi and back again. "That's good, right?" He laughed nervously. "I mean it would have to be. If we were in school, a ninety-two would be an A."

"Out here, it's more like a B-plus." Olivia draped her stethoscope across her neck and held on to the ends. "A reading in the high eighties to low nineties is good. If your levels drop below eighty-seven percent, we're in trouble."

"How much trouble?"

"You could be developing what's known as High Altitude Pulmonary Edema, commonly called HAPE."

"I can't pop a pill for that?"

Olivia shook her head. "There's nothing I can do. Not out here."

"What about steroids?" Gigi asked.

"They'd mask the symptoms, but they wouldn't treat the underlying cause. Plus I wouldn't want Chance to be linked to steroids because of something I prescribed. Medical reason or not, he'd never live down the stigma." Olivia addressed her fallen friend. "I'll take two more readings tomorrow, one while you're at rest and another while you're exerting yourself. If either of those readings is below ninety percent, congratulations. You win a trip down the mountain, a weeklong stay in the hospital, and a course of strong diuretics. And that's the best-case scenario."

Chance swallowed hard as the reality of the situation hit home. Then he sat ramrod straight. "I promised I'd make this journey with you and you know I never break my promises. When I leave this mountain, I'm walking off on my own two feet. I'm not getting carried off on my back."

"I want that for you, too," Olivia said, "but be smart, not stubborn. If your condition gets worse, you could die."

He looked frightened but tried to cover it with a smile that didn't quite reach his eyes. "Not gonna happen any time soon. I have way too much to live for."

Olivia wasn't swayed by his obvious attempt to charm her into telling him what he wanted to hear instead of what he needed to.

"Like I said, I'm going to give you another twenty-four hours. But you know your body better than I do. If something doesn't feel right between now and tomorrow, don't keep it to yourself. Let me or Gigi know ASAP. Deal?"

"You got it, Liv."

Sam heard a hint of resignation in his voice. He finally seemed to realize his fate didn't rest in his own hands. Out here, the mountain always had final say.

Gigi rubbed his shoulders. "Thanks, Olivia. I'll take it from here." Her voice was shaky, her eyes moist.

Chance patted her hands. "It's okay, *Mami*. A good night's sleep and I'll be as good as new. You'll see."

Gigi wiped away a tear. "Sleep is the poor man's medicine. The rich have better doctors."

Olivia squeezed her shoulder. "Remember that when I send you my bill." She closed her medical bag and stowed it in her backpack. Sam smiled to herself. She liked watching Olivia in action. She was a sight to behold. Gentle and kind but, at the same time, as tough as nails. What an intriguing combination.

Olivia zipped her backpack and slipped her arms through the straps. She turned suddenly, nearly catching Sam staring at her. The wind whipped her hair, lashed at her clothes. "Ready to go?" she asked, using an elastic band to corral her flyaway locks.

Sam nodded. She didn't trust herself to speak. If she did, she suspected she'd end up stammering like a smitten suitor or gushing like a starstruck fan. At the moment, she felt like both.

She resumed her slow but steady pace. When the group neared the fifteen thousand foot mark, she felt the first drops of rain splatter on her helmet. Jimmy and his assistants would have an easier time of it if they began setting up camp before the sky opened up. She was about to suggest they head back down the mountain when he flashed her a thumbs-up. They had been working together for so long they didn't need to talk to communicate. During climbs, they usually relied on hand signals or, like now, read each other's minds. Why couldn't she forge a bond like that with someone else? She had once. When it came to an end, she had resolved not to get that close again. She hadn't regretted that decision. Until last night.

Olivia held out her hand. Fat drops of rain pooled in her palm. "How long do the Sherpas need to set up?"

"Twenty minutes, give or take."

"Only five minutes per tent?" Olivia whistled in appreciation. "I need them to tag along with me the next time I go camping. I've never set up one tent in less than twenty minutes, let alone four." She studied the uneven terrain, carefully stepping around loose rocks. "You're not even breathing hard."

"I'm used to this."

"Or, like the Sherpas, are you too macho to let on how much you're hurting?"

Sam allowed herself a smile. "I thought you were a physician not a psychiatrist."

"I'm multi-talented."

"So I've noticed."

Olivia turned to look at her, but Sam remained focused on the trail. She didn't want Olivia to see the flicker of desire she felt burning in her eyes. A few minutes later, she gave Olivia a sidelong glance. Olivia looked remarkably fresh, but looks—even good ones—could be deceiving. Olivia easily mirrored her pace, a feat few clients had achieved, but the rest of the team was starting to fall behind. Sam took a quick assessment of the group and gave the signal to turn around.

Frowning, Olivia checked the altimeter on her watch. "We've only gone about fifteen hundred feet. I thought our goal for today was two thousand."

"It was, but your team's starting to drag. I think they've had enough for one day."

Olivia pursed her lips as if she intended to protest her decision. Sam had felt Olivia attempting to push the pace during the leg just as Jimmy said she had during the ascent to base camp. Sam had deliberately slowed the tempo whenever the gap between them and the rest of the group had grown too large. The first time it had happened, she had tried to laugh it off by asking, "What's the rush?" If it happened again, she wouldn't be nearly as nice.

Olivia was the kind of person who had to have her way at all times. She wasn't used to taking no for an answer. During an expedition, Sam was the same way. She knew in her gut she and Olivia were going to butt heads before the climb was over. Thankfully, the expected confrontation wasn't going to be today.

Olivia looked longingly at the trail, then shrugged and said, "Majority rules."

The team began to head back the way they had come. Peter slipped on the gritty trail, but Pasang grabbed a fistful of his jacket just before his feet went out from under him, saving him from a nasty fall.

"Thanks. I owe you one," he said gratefully. His hands shook from adrenaline. Or was it fear?

Pasang clapped him on the back. "Put it on my tab."

"Don't let your guard down," Sam said after she made sure Peter was okay. "No one ever fell *up* a mountain. Most accidents happen on the descent, not the climb."

Peter hurried to catch up to her and Olivia after they worked their way to the front of the pack. "I'd like to interview you for my vlog tonight."

"You already have more footage of me than you know what to do with," Olivia said.

"Not you." He turned to Sam. "You."

Sam was so surprised she nearly acted out the Jack and Jill nursery rhyme without the pail of water. "Why me?"

"The story is incomplete without your side of it." He framed an imaginary headline in the air. "'Heroic Guide Leads Team to Annapurna Peak.' Not my best, but you get the general idea."

Sam lengthened her stride, quickly establishing distance between herself and the rest of the pack. "Thanks, but no thanks. Pick someone else."

❖

In comparison to Mt. Everest, where permanent camps were virtual tent cities because of all the climbers conducting simultaneous assaults on the mountain, Annapurna I was barren. Four tents were erected in a circle. A fire pit had been dug in the center of the circle, but the rain, which had been falling nonstop for hours, prevented the gathered logs from catching fire. The only light and heat in the rapidly cooling darkness came from large Coleman lanterns. The supplies were housed in one tent. The climbers would share the other three. Olivia assumed the Sherpas would sleep in one; Gigi, Chance, and Peter in another; and she, Sam, and Marie-Eve would inhabit the third.

She balanced a plate of chicken fettuccine on her lap. The noodles were overcooked, the sauce was scalded, and the chicken tasted like the propane from the gas grill used to prepare the meal.

Marie-Eve, who had volunteered to make dinner, took a bite and frowned. "Sorry about the chow, guys."

Olivia shoveled another forkful into her mouth. She didn't care about the taste. She needed the protein. "It's hot and I didn't have to make it. That's all that matters."

Marie-Eve pushed her food around her plate. "Definitely not my best effort. Maybe I should stick to hockey."

"You'll do better the next time Pasang needs a day off." Olivia felt like a coach trying to lift a player's spirits after a bad game. "If not," she added with a wink, "you'll be relegated to KP for the rest of the trip."

She and her team sat shoulder to shoulder in a tent designed to sleep three. Space was limited, but the collected body heat helped her feel warm for the first time since they had stumbled into camp exhausted and soaking wet. She hadn't realized how tired she was until she stopped moving.

She listened to the rain falling against the rounded top and angled sides of the tent. The sound was so relaxing it nearly lulled her to sleep. Fatigue helped, too. She wasn't the only one feeling the effects of the "easy" first day. Yawns were frequent and prolonged.

Chance's persistent dry cough had not improved despite the lower elevation, but his breathing was markedly better and his appetite had returned. Both positive signs. She'd take as many of those as she could get.

Sam was right to end the leg when she had. Olivia patted herself on the back for picking the right guide—and tried to remind herself to stay out of the way so Sam could do her job.

Through the open tent flap, she could see Sam visiting with the Sherpas. Their tent was the largest of the four, a veritable Taj Mahal compared to the others. Only the supply tent, which housed both supplies and communications gear, approached its size. Sam sat on the tent floor. Her sinewy arms rested on her upraised knees, her triceps and forearms rippling as she opened a pack of beef jerky. Her black rain slicker was drying on the back of a rolled-up sleeping bag. If the sleeping bag was hers, she obviously intended to bunk down where she was instead of sharing a tent with her. *Looks like Marie-Eve and I will have the place to ourselves tonight.*

Peter jerked his chin in Sam's direction. "What was that about earlier?"

Olivia had a good idea what he was referring to, but she asked the question nevertheless. "What was what about?"

"She freaked out when I asked her to be in my vlog." He punched a series of buttons on the laptop Rae and Sam had provided. After Sam shot down his request for an interview, Olivia had stepped in to take her place. When he clicked Submit on the computer, their latest question and answer session was uploaded to his website, a spot visited by thousands of subscribers each day. "Maybe she has something to hide."

Olivia agreed Sam's adamant refusal was curious, but she doubted the snub warranted as much attention as Peter was giving it. "Contrary to popular belief, not everyone wants to have fifteen minutes of fame."

He pulled a lighter and a battered packet of Marlboros from the inner recesses of his water-resistant jacket. He shook out a cigarette and lit up. "I don't think the explanation is as simple as you're making it out to be. Anyone who climbs mountains for a living doesn't strike me as the shy, retiring type." He blew a smoke ring toward the tent opening. "I smell a story. I'm not going to stop digging until I unearth it."

"I smell smoke." Gigi fanned the air with both hands. "Could you hurry up and finish your cancer stick so the rest of us can breathe?"

"Let him enjoy it while he can," Chance said. "In another day or two, he'll have to choose between smoking and breathing. I think breathing will win out."

"Don't be so sure. Breathing can be vastly overrated, especially when I have this." Peter reached into his jacket and pulled out a plastic bag.

"Is that what I think it is?" Marie-Eve snatched the bag out of his hands, pulled it open, and stuck her nose inside.

"Friends have told me that they get the highest highs when they smoke at altitude."

"That's nothing more than a myth perpetuated by potheads attempting to swell their membership numbers," Gigi said.

Marie-Eve inhaled deeply. "And this is the finest weed I've ever come across." She zipped the bag shut and tossed it back. "When you dip into that, you'd better find me or else."

Peter stuffed the bag into his pocket. "Don't worry. I've got your back."

"I'm not even going to ask how you got that in the country," Olivia said.

Peter squirmed in his seat. "Let's just say I took one for the team."

The low rumble of laughter drew Olivia's gaze to the Sherpas' tent. Sam joined in the joviality as she unrolled her sleeping bag, but her eyes, lit by the flickering flame of the lantern at her feet, seemed haunted.

Sam looked up and met her gaze. Olivia offered what she hoped was a supportive smile. Sam's blank expression remained unchanged as she zipped the tent closed.

Peter extinguished his cigarette on the sole of his shoe and shoved the butt in his pocket. "Do you still think she doesn't have anything to hide?"

Olivia ate the last of her food, then rinsed her plate with the rest of her bottled water. "I think she has the right idea," she said with an exaggerated yawn. "Let's get some sleep so we can wake up and do this all over again tomorrow."

After everyone bedded down for the night, she was tormented by thoughts of something she couldn't explain. Sam was obviously holding something back, but Olivia couldn't imagine what. What secret was she hiding behind those blue eyes?

CHAPTER FOUR

Despite the guarantees of a certain red-haired orphan in a classic Broadway musical, the sun did not come out tomorrow. Or the day after. Or the day after that. The rain continued unabated for nearly four days. Hard at first, then a maddening drizzle that felt like an updated version of the ancient Chinese water torture. The treks uphill were slow going slogs, the ones downhill occasionally devolved into hair-raising slides. Mud covered everyone and everything.

"Tell me again why I decided to do this." Chance struggled to free his size fourteen hiking boots from the sodden earth.

"Because you didn't want me to have this wonderful adventure without you," Gigi said.

"By adventure, you mean—"

He didn't finish his sentence. His words trailed off as deep, racking coughs seized his body. He held an unsteady hand over his chest as if he were afraid of tearing something loose. The coughing fit continued for several minutes. When it finally ended, he took a deep breath and grinned as if to say, "I'm glad that's over." Then his eyes rolled back and he slowly toppled forward, crashing to the ground like a mighty oak being felled in a forest.

"Chance!" Gigi dropped her trekking poles and rushed to his side, half-crawling and half-sliding down the mountain. Olivia was right behind her.

Sam had been waiting for this to happen. Chance's blood oxygen levels had been hovering in the mid to high eighties since the morning after the first leg. High enough not to officially count as altitude sickness but too low for her comfort. She had to give him credit, though. He was a strong guy and he was fighting his heart out to keep inching his way up the mountain, but enough was enough. If Dr. Curtis didn't do what needed to be done, she'd pull the plug herself.

She roused him on the radio. "BC, do you read? Over."

"I'm here, Sam. What do you have? Over."

"A potential medical emergency. Be prepared to arrange evac. Stand by for further details. Over."

"Roger. Standing by. Over."

Olivia rolled Chance onto his back and stripped off her jacket. Rain quickly turned her long-sleeved white T-shirt transparent. The cotton cloth clung to her small, pert breasts and flat stomach. She tossed her jacket to Peter, who was standing slack-jawed a few feet away.

"What am I supposed to do with this?"

Olivia grabbed his pants leg and pulled him forward. "Keep the rain out of his face."

"Right." He and Marie-Eve held the jacket aloft like a protective tarp.

Forsaking modesty, Olivia peeled off her shirt, folded it up, and placed it under Chance's head. She gently disengaged Gigi's hands from his jacket. "Let me do my job, okay?"

"No!" Gigi pulled away. Her heartfelt pleas tore at Sam's heart. "Don't die, *Papi*. Don't die." She continued to claw at Chance's clothes, rub his cheeks. His unmoving face looked like a death mask. Blood seeped from his nose. Had he broken it during his fall or did he have yet another symptom of HAPE?

Olivia looked up, her eyes imploring. "Sam, help me."

Sam wrapped her arms around Gigi's shoulders and pulled her away. She strengthened her hold when the hysterical woman tried to break free. Gigi's sobs shook both their bodies.

Olivia wiped the caked-on mud off Chance's face and cleared his airways. She pressed her ear to his chest, then checked his pulse. "Persistent. Rapid. He's still with us."

"Oh, thank God."

Gigi sagged with relief. In an instant, Sam went from holding her back to holding her up. She tried and failed to find words of solace. Out of her element, she gave Gigi's shoulder an awkward pat.

"Jimmy, reach inside my backpack and toss me my—"

Anticipating her needs as well as he did Sam's, Jimmy handed Olivia her medical bag.

"Thank you."

"You're welcome, Dr. Bradshaw." He bowed and quickly backed away, giving her room to complete her assessment.

She waved smelling salts under Chance's nose. He groaned and jerked his head away from the pungent aroma.

"What the—"

When he tried to sit up. Olivia placed a hand on his chest and pushed him back down. "Easy."

He rested his head on the makeshift pillow. His eyes were wild. Filled with fear. Pink froth clung to his lips. His left hand scrabbled through the mud as if he were seeking to ground himself. Sam let go. Gigi crawled to her husband and held his hand in both of hers.

Awash in all-too-familiar feelings of helplessness, Sam sat on her haunches and watched the medical drama unfold.

Olivia stuffed a wad of cotton in Chance's nostril to staunch the flow of blood. Then she wrapped a blood pressure cuff around his arm. "Eighty over fifty. Too low," she said, more to herself than anyone else. She removed the cuff and placed the pulse oximeter on his index finger. Her shoulders sagged when the reading appeared on the small LED screen. "Sixty-eight. You know what this means, don't you?"

Chance nodded soberly. "A free ride down the mountain." He lifted his head and looked over his shoulder. The location for the second permanent camp was less than a ten-minute hike away, but he'd never reach it. Not on this trip, anyway. His first attempt to summit Annapurna I had come to an unceremonious end. "Do me a favor. Call a stretch limo, not a cab. I want to travel in style."

"Sure thing."

Olivia's face was wet. Sam couldn't tell if raindrops or tears were streaming down her cheeks. Olivia began to shiver. Her teeth chattered like castanets. Sam couldn't blame her. The rain felt like ice. If Olivia's body temperature fell too much, she'd have to treat herself for exposure.

Sam took off her jacket and draped it over Olivia's shoulders. Olivia continued working as if she didn't notice, but her hand brushed Sam's, her touch as soft as her whisper of thanks.

"We have a Gamow bag if you need it," Sam said.

Olivia's eyebrows knitted as she considered the suggestion. The pressurized compartment of the inflatable plastic chamber simulated the altitude at a lower elevation. Air introduced into the bag via a foot pump allowed the inhabitant's oxygen levels to return to a reading closer to normal.

"Keep it. The Gamow bag is for use in the most severe cases. We're not there yet." Olivia reached for a bottle of supplemental oxygen and placed the mask over Chance's face. "Keep this on. The extra O2 will help you breathe easier and keep you stable until you can receive more intense medical treatment in Kathmandu."

"Can you make it down on foot?" Sam asked.

With a shake of his head, Chance conceded defeat. "I don't think so."

Sam signaled for Tenzing and Mingma to retrieve the wheeled toboggan they would use to transport Chance back to base camp. Her gut had told her not to send Mingma home when Roland backed out of the climb. If she hadn't followed her instincts, she wouldn't have enough support personnel on hand to complete the expedition.

Tenzing and Mingma loaded Chance onto the toboggan and covered his long legs with a blanket. A small canopy protected him from the elements.

Peter and Marie-Eve drifted over to say good-bye and offer words of encouragement. Chance gave each a fist bump.

Tenzing and Mingma indicated they were ready.

"I'm going with you," Gigi said, continuing to hold Chance's hand.

He adamantly shook his head. "Don't give up on your dream because of me. I'll be in good hands." He pulled the oxygen mask aside to make sure his words were understood. "Stay and finish what you started."

Gigi tenderly but firmly replaced the mask. She placed one hand on Chance's chest and rested the other against his cheek. "I made a vow fifteen years ago and I don't intend to break it now. Wherever you go, I go with you."

Sam swallowed around the lump in her throat. She stepped away as Chance tried to plead his case. "But Olivia needs you to—"

Olivia spoke up. "I need two things: for you to get well and Gigi to make sure you do everything the doctors in Kathmandu tell you to. Do either of you have a problem with that?"

Chance grinned. "I'm not about to argue with one woman, let alone two."

Gigi kissed Olivia on both cheeks and held her close. "Be careful, Liv."

"I will."

"What about me?" Chance asked. "Don't I get any love?" When Olivia knelt and kissed his forehead, his broad smile quickly faded. "I'm sorry I let you down."

She squeezed his hand. "That's one thing you could never do."

He looked up at the mountain one last time. "I wish I could see the view from up there. You'll have to tell me all about it when you get home."

She kissed him again. "You'll be the first person I call."

She tried to stand, but he wouldn't let go of her hand.

"No matter what happens, this isn't on you, okay?" he said fervently. "It's on me. You didn't ask me to come. I volunteered. I knew the risks. Don't let anyone tell you otherwise. Especially you."

Sam could see Olivia's brave front begin to crumble. Her chin trembled as Chance struggled to sit.

"Finish the job," he said, carefully enunciating each word.

"I will. I promise." Olivia helped him settle back into a horizontal position. "Get well soon, okay? I wouldn't want my season tickets to go to waste."

"Not a chance."

Sam keyed the radio. "I've got two coming your way. One walking, one riding. Call emergency services and arrange chopper transport to Kathmandu for a case of HAPE."

"Ten-four," Dr. Curtis said.

After he signed off to place a call to Kathmandu on the sat phone, Rae's voice came on the radio. "What's the status of the rest of the party?"

"Shaken but holding it together. We're going to dry out in Camp Two for a few hours, then head down to Camp One to bunk for the night. Tomorrow's a rest day. That will give us a chance to regroup."

"How many porters do you have left?"

"Two, not including Pasang. Jimmy and Lhakpa are here with me. Tenzing and Mingma are on their way to you."

"Can you make it to the top with just three guys?"

"I've done it before with less."

"Not everyone climbs as well as you do."

Sam closed her eyes to guard against the unintended pain brought on by Rae's words. Memories flooded her mind at a time when she needed the distractions the least. She could still hear Bailey's voice. See the terror in her eyes. The same terror she had seen mirrored in Chance's. She dragged herself out of the past and focused on the task at hand.

"I'll keep you posted, Rae."

"I'll do the same. Over and out."

Sam knuckled away a tear.

You've never lost a client, she reminded herself. *And you're not about to start now.*

Olivia could use a hot bath and a good cry. She didn't have access to one and she couldn't afford the luxury of the other. Now, more than ever, her team needed her to lead them. She had to keep her shit together or the expedition that had been the most important item on her agenda for the past year would fall apart. She could handle the public humiliation if her mission failed, but she didn't know if she would be able to recover from the disappointment.

She cleaned up as best she could with facial cleanser, hand sanitizer, and biodegradable baby wipes, then slathered on deodorant. She slipped on jeans, a sweatshirt, and a pair of thick wool socks. Her hiking boots were still damp, but she put them on anyway.

"Better to have one pair of wet shoes than two."

Now that the rain finally seemed to be petering off, the temperatures were falling faster than the Dow Jones Industrial Average. It wouldn't take long for the wet ground to freeze.

Time to break out the crampons.

She smiled, remembering the bad joke Chance had made about crampons the day they arrived at base camp. Then she teared up, wishing he were still around to make even more. She was the team leader, but he was the official class clown. He had helped keep everyone loose. Without him around, would they break the tension or let it break them?

She hadn't received word of his condition. She had heard the chop of the rotors as the helicopter came in for a landing at base camp, but she hadn't heard anything else since Rae's brief message that the airlift was successful. That was hours ago. She had sent Gigi at least four text messages since then, but Gigi hadn't responded to any of them. Was she too busy to read the messages or too upset?

Olivia tried to curb the tendency for pessimism that often found her focusing on the dark cloud instead of the silver lining. She tried to remember what Chance had told her before he left. She had to finish the job. If she didn't, everything they had gone through would be in vain.

He had been so excited when she told him about the expedition. He had leaped at the chance to go with her before she could even ask the question. What if his playing career ended as a result of his condition? Despite what he had said, it wouldn't be on him. The blame would rest squarely on her shoulders. If he died, she didn't know if she could live with the guilt.

She closed her eyes.

Stop imagining the worst. Keep telling yourself everything will be fine and everything will be.

She picked up the jacket Sam had gallantly covered her with while she was treating Chance. She impulsively pressed the jacket to her nose. It smelled like Sam. Earthy yet ethereal. As solid as the ground beneath her feet but as light as the thin air in which she made a living.

"What are you doing?" Marie-Eve asked after she ducked inside the tent.

"Checking for B.O." Olivia draped the jacket over her arm. "I was about to return this to its rightful owner, but I wanted to make sure I didn't need to wash it first."

Marie-Eve snorted. "I think everything we own is wash and wear these days." She took a seat on her sleeping bag. "In case you're wondering, Peter's in charge of dinner tonight."

"If we keep this up, Pasang's going to think we don't like his cooking."

"He has nothing to worry about, believe me. Peter's trying to one-up me after my desultory effort on the first night. Admittedly, it wouldn't take much, but I'm half-hoping he falls flat on his face."

"What are we having?"

"Sausage, sauerkraut, and fried potatoes. For your sake, I hope this tent has good ventilation because my side of it is going to be gaseous tonight." Marie-Eve exchanged her light jacket for a heavier one. "You're single, aren't you, Doc?"

"Yeah. Why?"

"When this is over, I have a few friends I could introduce you to. You're what? Thirty-two? Thirty-three?"

"Thirty-five."

"You'd be perfect for my friend Soleil. She's twenty-three and she loves older women. I'll give you her number if you want to hook up when we get back to the real world."

"I don't think so." Olivia had never considered herself an older woman and didn't plan on starting now.

"Are you sure? Soleil's hot. I mean Angelina Jolie in *Tomb Raider* shorts hot."

"Then why aren't you with her?"

"Did I mention she was twenty-three?"

Olivia's life was complicated enough without adding an emotionally volatile twenty-three-year-old to the mix. The sex might be hot, but she didn't have time for the drama. Even though the attachments she formed were brief, they were with women who stimulated her intellectually as well as physically. Sam fulfilled both requirements.

Sam intrigued her. Olivia wanted to unravel the mystery behind those beautiful blue eyes—even while her tongue's caresses forced them to close.

"I'll see you at dinner," she said. "I'm going to ask Sam if she's heard any news about Chance."

"No news is supposed to be good news. I'll keep my fingers crossed."

"You and me both."

Sam's stomach growled. The smell of grilling bratwurst reminded her of Sunday afternoon tailgates outside the Metrodome. The Brett Favre era excluded, the Vikings had been so bad for so long the tailgate parties were often more enjoyable than the games. More competitive, too. She fought to overcome a wave of nostalgia. She didn't get homesick often, but when she did, the desire to return to life as she once knew it could be overwhelming.

A shadow loomed over the front of the tent. Sam observed the loose-limbed walk. The long, athletic strides.

"We've got company," Jimmy said in Nepali.

Sam responded in kind. "When are they going to realize they pay me to be their guide not their best friend?"

The figure raised a hand then lowered it. The body language was easy to read. *How do I make my presence known when there's no door to knock on and no bell to ring?*

Jimmy chuckled as he packed tobacco into his pipe. "Stop pretending you don't like your clients. You're a different person when they're around."

"Meaning?"

Sam pushed herself to her feet. Her head spun then cleared. She could already feel the effects of the altitude on her body. Her energy level was down and she had to concentrate to complete even the simplest tasks. Every exertion took extra effort—and required a longer recovery time. The group had been moving at a relatively brisk pace so far. Soon, though, their top speed would become a crawl.

Jimmy held a match to the bowl of the pipe and puffed his cheeks like a bellows until the tobacco leaves began to emit a thin trail of smoke. He waved his hand to extinguish the match. "When they're here, you have something to live for. Each time they leave, a little part of you goes with them."

"That's where you're wrong. Each time they leave, a little part of me comes back."

Maybe one day I'll be whole again.

"Yes, what is it?" She unzipped the flap and stepped outside, expecting to see Marie-Eve standing on her doorstep. "Oh, it's you."

Olivia stammered as if she was searching for what to say. "I—" She thrust a carefully folded bundle toward Sam. "Thanks for lending me your jacket."

"No problem." Sam caught a whiff of Olivia's distinctly feminine scent. A blend of daffodils and sunshine. Was the pleasant smell coming from Olivia or was her jacket infused with it? Sam wanted to wrap her arms around both. She held the jacket in front of her, placing a makeshift barrier between them. "How's the patient?"

"I haven't heard anything yet."

"No?" The chopper should have landed in Kathmandu over an hour ago. Sam thought Gigi would have sent Olivia a text message shortly after. Sam's heart went out to her. She could see her struggling to maintain her composure. The stress of the climb was clearly wearing on her. Watching her friend fall by the wayside surely didn't help. "I have contacts at the hospital where the chopper was headed. Let me make a few phone calls and see what I can find out."

"You'd do that?"

"Of course. Why wouldn't I?"

Olivia's expression grew even graver. "Because we're paying you to be our guide, not our best friend."

Sam's face burned from embarrassment. She felt like kicking herself. Olivia had researched Annapurna I so thoroughly she seemed to know every inch of the mountain. Why wouldn't she have studied the language, too?

Sam tried to clear the air. "That was—"

"Not meant for my ears so I'll pretend I didn't hear it."

If their positions were reversed, Sam didn't think she would have been nearly as gracious. She reached inside the tent and grabbed the satellite phone. "I'll let you know what I find out."

"I'd prefer to stay if that's okay with you."

"This could take a while. I wouldn't want you to miss dinner." She glanced at Peter and Pasang, who were loading steaming piles of food onto enamel plates.

"I'm not particularly fond of sausage."

Sam tried not to smile at the seemingly unintended double entendre. "Something we have in common."

She thought about grabbing her headlamp but quickly rejected the idea. The full moon overhead provided more than enough illumination. She examined the grayish black sky and winking canopy of stars. The clouds had cleared and she could see for miles. The view was spectacular. From the snow-capped mountain above to the lush valley and sparsely populated villages below.

She led Olivia to the supply tent and ushered her inside. If the news wasn't what Olivia wanted to hear, she should be allowed to react to it far from prying eyes.

She lit a lantern to chase away the darkness. Then she covered several pallets of canned goods with a sleeping bag liner to form a makeshift chair. "Not a Queen Anne, but the best I can do under the circumstances."

Olivia wordlessly took a seat.

Thirty minutes—and nearly as many miles of bureaucratic red tape later—Sam finally got the answers she was looking for.

"Did you follow any of that?" she asked after she ended the call.

Olivia leaned forward on her throne of beef stew and baked beans. Her hands were clasped between her knees as if in prayer. "I'm afraid I got lost the third time you were transferred."

Sam pulled up a "chair" of her own. "Long story short, everything's fine. Chance has been checked into the best hospital in Kathmandu and he has completed his first round of diuretics. Gigi hasn't called you back because she's sleeping as soundly as he is. He has a private room, but the hospital staff brought in another bed so she could stay after visiting hours. It was either that or watch her sleep on the floor."

Olivia laughed. Her rigid posture gradually relaxed as her tension slowly disappeared. "That's so like her. I knew she wouldn't leave his side for a second."

She sounded wistful. Almost envious. Was she wondering how it would feel to have someone love her that much?

"Thank you."

Sam tried to downplay her efforts. Her company's livelihood depended on successful summits and good word of mouth. She had spent half an hour talking to a parade of hospital personnel because she wanted to ease Olivia's mind, not because she wanted her to provide a glowing review after the expedition ended. "I didn't do anything."

"You did more than you know."

Olivia kissed Sam's cheek, then wrapped her arms around her neck with surprising strength. Sam didn't know whether to push her away or pull her closer. Frozen, she loosely held her in her arms and waited for her to let go. Only Olivia didn't let go. She clung to her like a drowning woman afraid of going down for the last time.

I'm probably supposed to hold her, but how? I'm probably supposed to say something, but what? She closed her eyes. *Don't think. Just do. Just...feel. Embrace your pain so you can help her let go of hers.*

Sam held on tighter, needing the contact as much as Olivia seemed to. For years, she had found comfort in the arms of strangers. How odd to be the one offering reassurance instead of the one seeking it.

"Go ahead," she whispered as Olivia began to cry. "Let it out if you need to. No one will think any less of you if you do."

How many times had she heard those same words? How many times had she wished she could take them to heart? As she stroked Olivia's hair—a gesture simultaneously familiar and foreign—she could sense Olivia trying to hold back. Trying to hold it together when what she needed most was to fall apart.

"Let it go, Olivia. I'm here."

Olivia stifled a sob and pushed her away. "I'm okay," she said, though Sam could see she was anything but. "Thanks for your help."

"No problem." Sam let her have the distance she seemed to crave. "If you need anything else, you know where to find me."

Olivia nodded and headed out of the tent. The sense of relief she felt was so great she didn't know whether to laugh or cry. Chance was going to be okay.

She joined Marie-Eve, Peter, and Pasang by the fire.

"Were you able to get an update?" Marie-Eve asked. She clapped her gloved hands after Olivia relayed the good news. "This calls for a celebration, don't you think?"

Peter reached into his bag of marijuana, pulled out a joint, and held the flickering flame of his lighter against the pointed tip. The distinctive smell of burning cannabis assaulted Olivia's nose. Peter took two puffs and passed the smoking joint to Pasang, who inhaled deeply before placing the thickly rolled cigarette between Marie-Eve's eager fingers.

"I never thought I'd hear myself say this, but this is better than sex," Marie-Eve said.

Peter retrieved the joint. "I'm glad you found a worthy substitute." He leaned over and shotgunned smoke into Pasang's mouth. The gesture was almost as intimate as a kiss. "Someone told me sex on the mountain is forbidden."

"No jiggy-jiggy," Pasang said, using one of the many Sherpa euphemisms for sex. "Sauce-making okay at base camp, maybe. On mountain, bring very bad luck. Mountain is to be respected and revered. She gets angry when she's dishonored."

"If she can hear the thoughts running through my head most nights," Marie-Eve said, "we're all in trouble."

Olivia jammed her hands into the pockets of her down parka. She felt like an overworked chaperone riding herd on a group of hormonal teenagers. She could use some adult conversation. Even if she was doing most of the talking.

"Would you like a hit, Doc?" Marie-Eve asked.

"No, thanks."

She didn't need to get high. What she needed, she realized with a start, was five more minutes in Sam Murphy's arms.

She had pulled away because the urge to stay had been too great. She didn't want to be seen as weak when everyone—herself included—needed her to be strong. Sam was her guide not her confidant. Their relationship, such as it was, needed to remain strictly professional. Olivia intended to keep it that way, even though her heart was beginning to long for more.

Chapter Five

Olivia's extremities felt like ice. She checked the thermometer propped against her backpack. According to the digital display, the temperature inside the tent was twenty-two degrees Fahrenheit. The air temperature outside was probably warmer but, thanks to the biting wind, it certainly wouldn't feel like it. Shivering, she pulled her sleeping bag up to her chin and moved closer to the warm body lying next to hers. The air was so cold she could see her breath. A thin layer of condensation had formed on the inside of the tent.

"Did you forget to close the flap when you turned in last night?"

Marie-Eve burrowed deeper into her own sleeping bag. Olivia could hear her teeth chattering. "No, did you?"

"I can't remember." She had barely been able to keep her eyes open by the time she had crawled into her sleeping bag last night. In her exhausted state, she might have neglected to secure the tent. Except when she checked it now, the flap was closed. She rolled over and pulled the zipper. Frigid air rushed inside.

"Brr. Damn, Doc. What did you do, forget to pay the heating bill?"

"The check's in the mail."

"That's what they all say." Marie-Eve disappeared inside her sleeping bag as if she were returning to the womb.

Olivia poked her head outside. Sparkling white snow—at least two feet by the looks of it—covered the ground. More continued to fall as huge flakes the size of dimes drifted from the sky.

"Wake up, Sleeping Beauty. You got your wish."

"Halle Berry's outside wearing nothing but lipstick and a smile?"

Olivia grabbed a handful of snow, squeezed it into a tight ball, and tossed it in Marie-Eve's direction.

Marie-Eve popped her head out of the sleeping bag. "I guess not." She vigorously shook melting ice and snow out of her hair before joining Olivia at the tent flap. Her eyes were bloodshot. She squinted to protect them from the blinding glare. "Looks like Christmas morning. But I suppose we should probably celebrate Halloween and Thanksgiving first, right?" She stuck her hand in the snow and whistled when her arm disappeared past the elbow. "If it's sticking this well down here, imagine how deep it must be farther up the mountain."

"It's gorgeous now, but we're going to be in for it once the temperature gets above freezing."

Living in a cold weather environment, Olivia was accustomed to seeing snow. What she could never get used to, though, was the mess the frozen precipitation caused once it began to melt. In Colorado, melting snow was an inconvenience. Out here, it could mean life or death. She hoped everyone had been paying attention during Sam's lecture on avalanche survival techniques. They might be putting her suggestions to use. Soon.

"Come on." She pulled cold weather gear out of her backpack. Thermal underwear, fleece-lined pants, wool socks, thick gloves, a wool cap, and her trusty down parka, in addition to gaiters and snowshoes. "The quicker we get dressed, the quicker we can get moving."

Marie-Eve returned to bed. "What's the matter? Got a hot date?"

Olivia finished dressing and waited in vain for Marie-Eve to begin. She nudged Marie-Eve's sleeping bag with the toe of her boot. "Up and at 'em. We need to get some food in our bellies before we hit the trail. You, Peter, and Pasang, especially. You have to get the marijuana out of your systems or today's leg could be ugly."

"Don't worry about us, Doc. We got the munchies so bad last night we ate six cans of beef stew between us. I probably have more preservatives in me than King Tut. You go ahead. I'll catch up in a bit."

Olivia pulled her cap over her ears and secured her helmet. "If you're not ready in thirty minutes, we're leaving without you."

Olivia climbed out of the tent and closed the flap. The camp seemed deserted, the only sounds the loud snoring coming from Marie-Eve's and Peter's tents. The Sherpas' tent was empty, their bedrolls and belongings nowhere to be found. Food and coffee warmed over the campfire, which sputtered but continued to burn.

Olivia saw Sam exit the supply tent. Her clothes were wrinkled and her short hair was wild. She looked as if she had tossed and turned all night, though Olivia couldn't imagine why. Sam combed her hair with her fingers before covering her unruly locks with her helmet. She looked around, taking the lay of the land. Olivia had been astonished to wake up and discover the mountain had turned into a winter wonderland overnight, but Sam's face betrayed no hint of surprise. As if she had seen it all before. Then again, she probably had.

Olivia poured herself a cup of coffee from the metal pot hanging over the campfire. The thick brown liquid woke her and warmed her at the same time. "Would you like some?" she asked when Sam joined her by the fire.

"Yes, please." Olivia poured her a cup and returned the container to the hook attached to a metal crossbeam. Sam took the cup from her and inhaled half the contents. Then she peeked inside a cast iron pot, revealing bacon, poached eggs, and home fries. "Would you like some breakfast?"

Olivia was too upset over Chance's departure to eat, but she knew she had to force something down or risk running out of gas on the trail. "Please."

Sam grabbed two plates and loaded them with food. She and Olivia sat on opposite sides of the fire. They didn't talk, but the silence felt comfortable instead of strained.

"Where's everyone?" Olivia eventually asked.

"Jimmy and the guys are climbing ahead."

"Are they attaching fixed ropes?"

Fixed ropes performed the same function as a hand railing attached to a flight of stairs. Providing support and reassurance, they were bolted to mountains to assist climbers and trekkers as they made their way over particularly difficult sections. Adventurers clipped one end of a climbing tool called an ascender to the rope and attached the other end to the harness around their waists, then hung on for dear life.

"We won't need fixed ropes until we climb from Camp Two to Three. Then the elevation becomes much more challenging. Jimmy, Pasang, and Lhakpa are scouting the trail to make sure the snow isn't camouflaging any potential danger zones. If any new crevasses have formed since the last time we reconnoitered the area, chances are we wouldn't see them until we fell through the opening."

Olivia shuddered at the thought of stepping onto what she thought was solid ground only to find nothing more substantial than snow and air beneath her and a long, potentially fatal fall.

Sam scraped the last bite of food off her plate and cleaned the smooth stainless steel surface with fresh snow. Then she downed the rest of her coffee and dashed the paltry remainder on the ground. "Is your crew prepped and ready to go?"

"Almost." Olivia poured two more cups of coffee, one each for Marie-Eve and Peter.

"Get them ready. We need to start climbing as soon as we can in case there's more weather on the way."

Sam grabbed a shovel and began dumping snow on the fire. While she waited to see if the flames had been extinguished, she held the last shovelful of snow aloft. Olivia marveled at her strength. How was she able to keep her arms from trembling under the heavy weight? The woman was practically a machine.

She had developed her muscles in the gym, spending as much time as possible in the hospital fitness center between rounds. Sam had apparently earned hers the old-fashioned way. Through hard work.

"Sam." Jimmy's voice came over the walkie-talkie, panicked and reedy.

Sam stuck the blade of the shovel in the snow and reached for the walkie-talkie clipped to her waistband. "I read you, Jimmy," she said in Nepali. "What's wrong?"

"We've found something."

"Something like what?"

Sam cast a wary eye at Olivia as she waited for Jimmy's reply. When it came, Olivia's brain was too muddled to translate what he said. It was way too early and she hadn't had nearly enough caffeine. Had he found a *bhatti* or a body? Neither made sense. Sixteen thousand feet was too high for a tea stall and too low for a corpse. Theoretically. On Annapurna I, anything was possible.

The grim expression on Sam's face let Olivia know the correct answer, unfortunately, was the latter.

"Can you tell who it is?"

"The Sri Lankan who tried to climb the mountain solo. The one who went up last April and never came down."

Sam looked stricken. "Sanath? Are you sure it's him?"

"The St. Christopher medal he wore is still around his neck."

"Can you tell what happened?"

"It appears a large rock came off the mountain and crushed his skull. Half his head is caved in. We found his helmet farther up the mountain. It was undamaged so I don't think he was wearing it at the time of his accident. He also fell a great distance. I'd say at least a thousand meters. His neck is broken and the bones in his arms and legs are like powder."

Olivia grimaced. She knew from treating patients that the pain from a broken bone was excruciating. Multiple fractures must have been unbearable. She hoped Sanath's death had been swift and immediate.

"That makes no sense. Wearing a helmet is Climbing 101. There's no way he would have made such a rookie mistake. I taught him better than that."

"I can't explain what happened, Sam. I can only tell you what we found. After Lhakpa and I bring the body down, should we send him home or bury him in a crevasse? You knew him better than I did. What do you think he would have wanted?"

Marie-Eve crawled out of the tent. Olivia shook her head when she started to speak. Frowning, Marie-Eve looked from Olivia to Sam and back again. "What's going on?" she whispered.

"Jimmy found the remains of a missing climber," Olivia whispered back. She handed Marie-Eve the cups of rapidly cooling coffee she forgot she had been holding. "He and Sam are trying to decide what to do with the body. It's tradition for someone lost on a mountain to be buried on the mountain, but he's been missing for so long his family might want a chance to say good-bye without having to fly two thousand miles to do it."

Stunned into silence, Marie-Eve gulped as she looked off into the distance. "This is a beautiful resting place, but I don't want it to be mine."

Neither did Olivia, but the possibility that it could happen had never seemed more real. Sanath had many more climbs under his belt than she did. If such an experienced climber could have a fatal accident, no one was safe.

Sam pinched her eyes shut with her left hand. Tears leaked between her fingers. The machine was human after all.

Sam abruptly turned her back as if she suddenly remembered she had an audience. An audience she didn't want to perform for. "He's a climber. He'd want to stay here. We can lay him to rest in one of the crevasses between Camps One and Two."

Olivia remembered the gashes in the earth Sam was referring to. One was so deep her legs had refused to obey her brain's commands when she crawled over the metal ladders that had been strung across it.

"Give us some time to wrap the body in plastic sheeting and prepare it to be moved," Jimmy said. "Find some spare tarp we can use as a coffin. We'll see you in about an hour."

Sam signed off and clipped the walkie-talkie to her waistband. She took a few moments to gather her composure before she turned around. "Jimmy, Lhakpa, and I have to descend to Camp One to—"

"We heard," Olivia said gently.

Sam's chin trembled. She looked away as her eyes filled with tears. Olivia sensed Sanath wasn't the only person she was mourning. Sam had never lost a client, but perhaps she had lost someone even more precious. After a few seconds, she cleared her throat and resumed speaking. "Pasang will lead you to Camp Three so you can begin acclimatizing. The rest of us will sleep at Camp One tonight and catch up to you tomorrow."

"Peter and Marie-Eve can go with Pasang, but I'm coming with you," Olivia said. "Even though I didn't know Sanath, I'd like to pay my respects. I can see how much he meant to you. Let me help you say good-bye."

Sam, her bright eyes dulled by pain, approved Olivia's request with a nod.

"Did you know him well?" Olivia asked.

"The group of dedicated climbers is a small one. We're members of an exclusive club, each member racing to be the first to achieve a goal. Of course we all know each other." Despite her heretofore laconic demeanor, Sam seemed to welcome the opportunity to talk. "I met him five years ago when we were in the same group that climbed Kilimanjaro. I thought he seemed sincere, if a bit reckless, but his passion for climbing impressed me. He became a friend and something of a protégé. I greeted him at the airport when he landed in Kathmandu last spring. We shared a couple beers and shot the breeze for a few hours before we caught a chopper to the Conservation Area. Before we parted ways, I told him the next round was on me when he made it back. Only he never made it back."

Sam's voice broke as she finished her story.

Peter had wandered out of his tent sometime during Sam's tale. "What did I miss?" he asked as Marie-Eve handed him a cup of cold coffee.

"I'll fill you in later." She extended her hand. "I'm sorry for your loss."

"Thank you."

"Didn't anyone notice Sanath was missing?" Olivia asked after Peter and Marie-Eve returned to their tents to prepare for their ascent to Camp Three.

"His base camp manager got nervous when she lost radio contact with him sometime during the second week of his climb. Searchers went up the mountain, but they couldn't find any trace of him. Crevasses open and close depending on the movements of the glaciers near them. Sanath's body must have come to rest in one that later closed then opened up again, allowing flood waters from the monsoons to dislodge his body and his belongings from their hiding place."

"Why do you think he wasn't wearing his helmet?"

"Like I said, he could be reckless and altitude makes you do strange things. That's why no one should ever attempt a feat of this magnitude alone. You need someone to keep you in check when you aren't able to do it yourself. Even if you think you know what's best, there's always someone who knows better."

Olivia heard what Sam had left unsaid. Sanath's fate could befall her if she took similar risks. But she could see the determination in Sam's eyes to prevent that from happening to her or anyone else. She realized the reason Sam put her life at risk every day. To prevent others from losing theirs.

Though she was standing on the world's most dangerous mountain, Olivia had never felt so safe.

The rope dug into Sam's palms as she, Olivia, and Lhakpa slowly lowered Sanath's body into the crevasse. Jimmy presided over the informal ceremony. He held up a piece of white cloth, making an offering on behalf of the dead. His sweet, melodic voice rose to the heavens as he recited the *mataka-vastra-puja*.

"Impermanent alas are formations, subject to rise and fall. Having arisen, they cease; their subsiding is bliss."

Sam let go of her end of the rope after Sanath's body settled onto the bottom of the crevasse. She poured water into an overflowing cup, a task she performed in Sanath's family members' absence. "As water raining on a hill flows down to the valley, even so does what is given here benefit the dead. As rivers full of water fill the ocean full, even so does what is given here benefit the dead."

Lhakpa kneeled at the edge of the deep fissure. He wriggled the ropes free, then took aim and dropped a burning torch onto the propane-drenched tarp that covered Sanath's body. The resulting fireball was so powerful the percussion forced everyone to take a step back. Thick, acrid smoke poured out of the hole. Olivia said a quick prayer then rushed to get downwind. She covered her nose and mouth with her jacket to guard against the sickly-sweet smell.

Sam clutched Sanath's St. Christopher medal. A fan had presented it to him after his successful solo ascent of K2. Even though he was Buddhist, not Catholic, Sanath had worn the talisman every day since. It had accompanied him on successful climbs around the world. It had been with him at the end.

The horrible thing was his death could have been prevented if he had only followed the precautions Sam had tried to drill into him. Had she been wasting her breath? Why hadn't he listened?

She ran her finger over the medal's raised surface. "Safe journey, my friend. May your next life be as exciting as this one." Except for memories and photographs, the talisman would be the only thing his friends and family would have to remember him by.

Jimmy held his fur hat in his hands. Lhakpa did the same. Their short black hair fluttered in the breeze. "I'll radio Rae so she can arrange for a monastic to visit his survivors and perform the *mataka-bana* at the appropriate time."

In three days, a clergyman would visit Sanath's relatives and neighbors and give an hour-long sermon on his behalf.

"Thank you, Jimmy." Sam held up the St. Christopher medal. "Please let his mother know I'll bring this to her as soon as I can."

"Of course." Jimmy pressed his palms together and placed his hands under his chin. "*Namaste*, Sam. Dr. Bradshaw."

Sam turned to Olivia after Jimmy and Lhakpa returned to Camp One. "Thank you, too. You weren't obligated to take part in this ceremony, but I'm glad you were here."

"Please don't thank me. I participated because I wanted to not because I had to. I'm just glad I could do my part. How are you feeling?"

Sam felt raw. An old wound had been ripped open, and she felt the pain as acutely as she had the first time around.

When she climbed into her bedroll tonight, she knew she wouldn't be able to sleep. When she closed her eyes, all she would be able to see was the look of horror on Bailey's face. All she would be able to hear were her screams. All she would be able to think about was that day. That one fateful day on Mont Blanc.

But she didn't want to talk about that day. She wished she could stop reliving it. No matter how many times she replayed it in her mind, the end result never changed.

No matter how many people she saved, she couldn't make up for the one she had lost.

"I feel better, thanks."

Sam looked at the ground. The path was relatively clear, this part of the mountain having received only a light dusting of snow. If the clouds overhead were any indication, however, the higher elevations would receive several feet before this latest system moved on its way. The iffy weather afforded her the perfect reason to stop thinking about life and death and focus on work.

"I'd better ask Rae to check the radar and give us a report. Jimmy will never think to do it. Thank you again. Your efforts were much appreciated."

She turned to head back to camp.

"Sanath isn't the only person you're mourning, is he?"

Taken aback by Olivia's perceptiveness, Sam stopped walking. She didn't turn around, though. She didn't think she could bear to face the tenderness she suspected she'd see in Olivia's eyes. She didn't want anyone to care about her. She didn't want anyone to love her. Not that way. Not ever again.

"When you lose someone, it helps to talk about them," Olivia said. Sam could hear—could *sense*—her moving closer. When she spoke again, she was so close Sam could feel the heat radiating from her body. "I know how much it hurts. I lost my father when I was young. He was my hero. The greatest man I've ever known. We did everything together. I was inconsolable when he died. The only thing that helped me get over the loss was listening to other people's stories about him. Sharing all the memories we created." Olivia came closer still. "If you want to talk, I'm willing to listen."

Olivia gave her shoulder a squeeze, then stepped around her and walked away. Sam watched her go. She had tried sharing her story before, but rehashing the details of the worst day of her life hadn't taken away the pain. Perhaps she had chosen the wrong audience. And perhaps she had finally found the right one.

Was Dr. Olivia Bradshaw the woman who could heal her broken heart and shattered soul? There was only one way to find out, but she didn't know if she was ready to take the chance.

❖

Sam collected the trash from dinner—heavy-duty plastic pouches that had once contained roast beef, potatoes, carrots, and dinner rolls.

Olivia wiped crumbs off her lips. Her body hummed with the influx of sugar. She had been craving gooey, decadent desserts for days. The fudge brownie in the dessert pouch was just what the doctor ordered. "My compliments to the chef."

"Save the kind words for someone who deserves them. Even I can't screw up an MRE."

Sam's response was as gruff as ever, but the corner of her mouth lifted into a smile. She still seemed to carry a psychic burden, but finding closure with Sanath appeared to have eased the load.

From the day they met, Sam had seemed almost superhuman. Now that she had proven herself to be mortal after all, Olivia was more drawn to her than ever. She wanted to share the weight that caused Sam's shoulders to slump and her eyes to dim. She wanted to put the light back in those eyes.

She gave herself a mental shake. This wasn't like her. She had signed up for an adventure with the hope of a few fringe benefits, not happily ever after. Yet here she sat mentally packing a U-Haul and practically setting up house.

Even though she had taken scores of risks in her life, there was one she hadn't tried. She had never allowed herself the time to fall in love. Sam made her want to slow down long enough to give it a chance.

But she couldn't slow down. Not when there were still so many things she wanted to accomplish. Her father had died relatively early. If she followed suit, she wanted to be sure she left a legacy behind. Love could wait.

"What time are we leaving to join the others?" she asked.

"According to the weather report, tomorrow's going to be a warm one. If we leave at four a.m., we'll be well on our way before the sun starts beaming down in earnest."

"Then I'd better hit the hay." Night fell unnaturally early on the mountain. Without looking at her watch, Olivia couldn't tell if it was closer to noon or midnight. "If I turn in now, perhaps I won't be quite as crabby as I usually am at the ass crack of dawn."

"Do you mind if I tag along? Jimmy might not say much when he's awake. In his sleep, he talks a blue streak."

Lhakpa nodded enthusiastically. "Talk, talk, talk all night long," he said in heavily accented English.

"At least I don't twitch in my sleep. As many punches as you throw, I'm surprised you haven't given me a black eye by now. When I go home at the end of this trip, my wife's going to think I was attacked by a Yeti."

Jimmy's comments sparked a good-natured argument between the pair about who was the greater offender. An argument that grew louder and more comical by the minute.

"Do you see what I have to put up with?" Sam asked as Jimmy and Lhakpa continued to bicker.

Olivia laughed, enjoying the unexpected moment of levity. "You're right. No one should be subjected to that."

She beckoned for Sam to follow her. After they ducked inside the tent, Sam secured the flap. Then she unrolled her sleeping bag and crawled inside. Olivia took off her boots and slipped inside her own sleeping bag. An inflatable mattress rested between it and the hard, unforgiving ground. When Sam switched off the lantern, Olivia struggled to adjust to the sudden darkness. Then she closed her eyes and tried to sleep. Little by little, her body gave in to fatigue. She began to drift off.

"How old were you when you lost your dad?"

Sam's question was startling in both its directness and its simple curiosity. Olivia struggled to lift her heavy lids. She wanted to be awake enough to give the question the well-formed response it deserved.

"I was eleven, but I remember it like it was yesterday. It was a Saturday morning in September. The first day of college football season. The Buffaloes were scheduled to play the Texas Longhorns at home. We had tickets on the fifty-yard line. Mom was in the kitchen packing a picnic lunch to take to the game. I was in my room trying to decide if I should wear my black U of C sweatshirt or my gold one. Dad was in the den reading the paper and listening to the pre-game show on the radio."

She closed her eyes as she pictured the scene.

"We lived within walking distance of the stadium so we never drove unless the weather was really bad. Whether we were walking or driving, Dad insisted on being in his seat in time to see the teams run through warm-ups. He kept us on a strict schedule to make sure he didn't miss a single jumping jack or stretching drill. He'd stand by the front door and yell out updates. 'This is your thirty-minute warning.' 'This is your fifteen-minute warning.' When it was time to go, he'd let out a piercing whistle that drove all the dogs in the neighborhood crazy. 'All right,' he'd say. 'Fall in or fall out.'"

She chuckled at the memory, but her laughter quickly faded.

"That day, though, the updates never came. I didn't think anything of it when Dad didn't give the thirty-minute warning—I was too busy gabbing on the phone with a girl I had a crush on to notice much of anything. When he didn't give the fifteen-minute warning, I finally realized something was amiss. My mom was too busy to notice, but I did. In case I was wrong, I didn't want to alarm her. I hung up the phone and went downstairs to the den. I found Dad sitting in his favorite chair. He seemed unnaturally still. I called his name, but he didn't respond. The paper was on his lap, the radio was on. When I touched him, he was still warm. His eyes were open, but he was gone. He'd had an aortic aneurysm brought on by an undiagnosed heart ailment. The paramedics said the rupture was so catastrophic that, even if the vessel had burst while he was on the operating table, the surgeons wouldn't have been able to save him."

"How old was he?"

"Forty-one. Only six years older than I am now."

"That explains why you drive yourself so hard." Sam's sleeping bag rustled. Olivia thought she was settling in for the night until she asked her another question. "Did losing your father prompt you to become a doctor, so you could save those no one else thinks can be saved?"

Olivia carefully considered the question. "Yes and no." She wasn't bold enough to consider herself a miracle worker, even though others might see her that way.

"My father lived in one of the most technologically advanced countries in the world, but he didn't take advantage of it. He was the kind of guy who went to the doctor only if he absolutely had to because he thought most of them were quacks or pill pushers. I wanted to erase that stigma. I wanted to make medical care more accessible and less frightening. Some patients shake in their boots the first time they see me coming. It's my job to help them realize I'm there to help them not hurt them. I don't want anyone to feel as helpless as I did the day my father died. I want to make my dad proud of me. That's why I became a doctor."

"You're smart, level-headed, and successful. I think your dad would be proud. Any parent would be if they had a daughter like you."

Olivia was flattered yet embarrassed by the praise. "I'm sure your family is equally proud of your accomplishments if not more so."

"My family loves me unconditionally. I just wish I deserved it."

Olivia didn't know how to respond to Sam's statement. How could someone who had as many things going for her as Sam did not feel worthy of love?

"You were right earlier," Sam said quietly. "Sanath wasn't the only person I was mourning today. I was mourning Bailey, too."

She paused as if she was unsure whether to continue. Olivia willed herself to have the patience to wait for her to make up her mind.

"Losing your dad is the reason you became a doctor," Sam said at last. "Losing Bailey is the reason I became a guide."

"Tell me about her."

Sam took a deep breath and began to tell the story of her life. The story of her lover's death.

CHAPTER SIX

I met Bailey when I was twenty-two. She introduced me to climbing and I got hooked on it."

Sam remembered the twin thrill of simultaneously discovering something she had an affinity for and someone with whom she could share the experience. Meeting Bailey had felt right. It had felt like fate. Unfortunately, fate had taken a tragic turn. She sighed and forced herself to continue telling a story she had shared with only a relative few.

"Within a year, we progressed from climbing rock walls to climbing mountains. Easy ones at first, then more challenging ones. Climbing was easy for me. It was intuitive. Instinctive. I didn't have to think. I could just see the path I was supposed to take. Bailey's style was more workmanlike. When it was her turn to act as team leader, she'd study the mountain and research previous ascents before settling on the one she thought was best."

"Isn't that what you did for this expedition?" Olivia asked. "I saw you researching the day before we started out."

"When people's lives are on the line, I don't like to leave anything to chance. My style is too much of a risk."

"It sounds like a risk worth taking. To fly by the seat of your pants, relying solely on your own instincts."

Sam heard the excitement in Olivia's voice. A love of adventure and a willingness to try anything new. The quality was intoxicating, but a bit frightening, too. How could she keep Olivia safe when she was so eager to put herself in danger?

"For my twenty-fifth birthday, Bailey surprised me with two tickets to France. I thought we'd spend two weeks sunning on the beach in St. Tropez, but she said she wanted to climb Mont Blanc. Even though it tops out at less than sixteen thousand feet, Mont Blanc is the tallest mountain in Western Europe. Annapurna I has a higher percentage of fatalities, but Mont Blanc has a larger number. On average, fifty people die there a year."

"What makes it so deadly?"

"The mountain is short with a broad base. It's an easy climb, which is why so many people flock to it, but not all those hoping to ascend are savvy enough to recognize the warning signs or take heed of their own limitations. They buy the equipment, watch a couple of videos, and think they're properly prepared to do what needs to be done. They couldn't be more wrong. They get swallowed up by avalanches or crevasses, struck by falling spears of ice, or felled by dumb luck or their own inexperience."

"But you and Bailey were experienced climbers."

"Not experienced enough. From the time we landed in France, I felt like we had a dark cloud hanging over us. Because we were in over our heads and I knew it. Mont Blanc is a test of climbers' ice climbing skills. As you'll see when we get to the ice wall, ice climbing is vastly different from regular climbing. When ice climbing, you work in teams of two and you're tethered to your partner. The lead climber paves the way. It's her responsibility to place ice screws and thread a rope between them to establish support points. The second climber removes the screws on her way up. If the second climber slips, the rope and the lead climber will stop her fall. The lead climber doesn't have that security. She has only the ice screws to depend upon. If she falls before she can establish both support points, she has no chance to recover. The second climber has to hold on and hope the force of the lead climber's fall doesn't pull her down as well. That's why the stronger climber usually takes the lead. If both climbers aren't equally skilled, there could be trouble."

"So Bailey took the lead on Mont Blanc?"

"Yes. I wanted to say no—I should have said no—but she was so excited, I went along with her plan. She didn't say it, but I could tell she felt overshadowed by my success. She introduced me to climbing, but I was better at it. The pupil had outshined the teacher. Deep down, I think she felt Mont Blanc represented her opportunity to even the playing field. So I said yes."

"Do you think the outcome would have been different if you hadn't?"

"I asked myself that every minute of every day for years. Then I finally realized I can't change history. I can only do my best to prevent it from repeating itself."

"Is that why you're here with me?"

Sam felt like she and Olivia were fated to cross paths, but she was still waiting to see what fate had in store this time around.

"Despite my misgivings, the Mont Blanc climb began auspiciously. On the first leg, we climbed over glaciers and some amazing formations that looked like boulders made of ice. They were formed when ice melted, made its way down the mountain, and later solidified. On the third day, we reached the Gervasutti Couloir, a narrow canyon that tests the mettle of even the most skilled climbers. The ascent was tough—tougher than any I'd made at that point. My arms were burning and I wasn't the one doing the hard work. When I asked Bailey how she was doing, she said she was fine, but I could tell she was hurting. We had two choices: keep climbing or accept defeat and take the cable car back to camp. We kept climbing."

"What happened?" Olivia asked as if Sam was taking too long to get to the point.

"Six hundred feet from the top, I thought we were going to be okay. I thought all my worrying had been for naught. We were almost there. Almost home." Sam paused to gather the energy she needed to tell the hardest part of the story. "Then Bailey slipped. She was ten yards ahead of me. I saw it happen, but there was nothing I could do to stop it."

Olivia's shocked gasp echoed off the walls of the small tent. Sam focused on technique so she could keep her roiling emotions in check.

"When you climb glaciers, you have an ice axe in each hand. You 'swim' up the mountain, stroking with one hand then the other as you drive the point of your axe into the ice. You're supposed to wait until your ice axe is secure before you make the next stroke. Bailey didn't wait. She had established a rhythm and she ended up hypnotized by it. She swung the axe with her right hand and automatically raised her left. The ice cracked underneath her axe. She tensed when she heard the sound. Her foot slipped and the ice gave way. Chunks the size of softballs pelted my helmet. One hit me so hard I saw stars. Dizzy and disoriented, I ducked my head until the barrage was over."

"It's okay," Olivia said, breaking in. "You don't have to tell me the rest."

"I know," Sam said, "but I want to. I want you to know why I do the things I do. Why I say the things I say. Why—" She faltered. "Why I'm the way I am."

"Okay. Tell me."

"Bailey tried to dig her crampons into the ice, but we were on a sharply-angled vertical and she didn't have the strength to lift her legs high enough to regain her foothold. Her feet fell away from the wall and she lost her grip on the ice axe in her left hand. She dangled from the wall, all her weight on one axe."

She felt Olivia's hand on her arm, offering much-needed comfort.

"I was at the end of the rope—a good thirty feet away. When my head cleared a bit, I yelled at Bailey to hold on. I told her I was coming to get her. I asked her to wait for me. When she looked down at me, I could see the fear in her eyes. She told me to hurry."

Sam remembered the sudden rush of adrenaline that had surged through her battered body.

"I've never climbed so fast in my life. But I wasn't fast enough. The ice cracked again and she started to fall. Even though it took only a few seconds for her to pass me, it seemed to take an eternity."

Olivia gripped her arm tighter. Sam could feel Olivia's strength flowing into her, easing the heavy burden her heart continued to carry.

"I dug my feet into the ice and reached for her. I knew my ice axe wouldn't support our combined body weight for long, but all I needed was a minute or two. Time enough for Bailey to find purchase. I held my hand out to her. She lunged for me. Her fingers brushed against mine, but I couldn't get close enough to latch on to her. The rope was out of reach as well. I've never prayed so hard to be just a couple of inches taller. My prayers weren't answered. One second, Bailey was above me. The next, she was below me and falling fast. When I knew I couldn't stop her fall, I held on and waited for her weight to pull the rope taut. I waited for her to find her way back on the mountain or pull me off with her. The tug never came. Because Bailey did something remarkable. Before the rope played out, she reached for the carabiner attached to the belay loop on her climbing harness. I screamed at her to stop, but she didn't."

"No," Olivia whispered in the dark.

"She told me she loved me, then severed the connection between us. It was twenty-seven hundred feet to the bottom of the canyon. My screams followed her the whole way down, preventing me from hearing the sickening thud when her body hit the ground. I was tempted to take the same route she did and follow her down, but I wasn't brave enough to do it. I managed to descend low enough to catch the cable car. By the time I reached the bottom of the canyon, officials from the mountain rescue station had already recovered her body. Through my tears, I had to identify her remains."

"I can't imagine having to do something like that alone so far from home. So far from the ones you love."

"But I was with the one I loved the most," Sam said. "I had to do it. For her. I still can't get over the look on her face. She was scared when she slipped—anyone would have been—but when she unclipped herself from the rope, she looked like she was at peace with her decision. She looked the same way at the mountain rescue center when the officials uncovered her face so I could confirm the body they found was hers."

Sam dried her eyes. She could never tell the story without crying. She was surprised she had made it this far before her tears had begun to flow.

"Calling her parents was the hardest thing I've ever had to do. Even though the trip was her idea, her folks blamed me for the accident. Her mother said what happened was my fault. Her father said if I hadn't met her, she'd still be alive."

"That's harsh."

"They didn't say anything I hadn't already said to myself."

"What happened when you got home?"

"Life as I knew it was over so I tried to begin a new one. I packed my bags and set off with no real destination in mind. I bummed around Mexico for a while, working at bars and tourist hotels until I scraped up enough money to return to Europe. I missed climbing. No matter how hard I tried to stay away, I couldn't resist the pull. I couldn't let Mont Blanc beat me. I couldn't let it beat us. I climbed it with a picture of Bailey in my pocket. When I reached the top, I planned to say good-bye to her. To finally lay her memory to rest. But when I reached the summit, I couldn't let go. The weight I'd been expecting to fall from my shoulders got heavier instead of lighter. So I kept moving. I kept climbing. Thinking if I just got high enough, I'd find what I was looking for. I'd find peace. I'd find forgiveness. I guess I haven't gotten high enough yet because I'm still looking for both. Bailey gave her life to save mine. For the longest time, I couldn't forgive her for it. Then I couldn't forgive myself. As the stronger climber, I should have taken the lead that day."

"You hold yourself responsible for what happened? You blame yourself for Bailey's death?"

"She loved me enough to make the ultimate sacrifice. If I had protected her as well as she protected me, she'd still be alive."

Olivia had listened mostly in silence while Sam unraveled the mystery of her past, but she could remain silent no longer.

"We may seem different, but you and I have something in common. We are who we are because of who we've lost and the way we've lost them. What happened to Bailey wasn't your fault. You refer to it as an accident—unconsciously or not—because that's what it was. A terrible, unfortunate accident." She tried to keep her voice gentle. Sam needed understanding, not criticism. "Yes, there are things you could have done. There are also things she could have done. But it's too late to ask yourself 'What if?' Bailey's gone. Not because of what you did or didn't do, but because accidents happen. No matter how well you might prepare for any eventuality, accidents happen."

Sam sniffled. Olivia needed to see her face. This wasn't the kind of conversation you conducted under the cover of darkness. It was the kind of conversation you had while looking into each other's eyes.

She fumbled for the lantern. She turned it on its lowest setting and squinted as the feeble light chased away the gloom.

Tears glistened on Sam's cheeks. When Sam moved to wipe them away, Olivia grabbed her hand. "You've shared so much with me today. Don't hide now." She touched a faint scar on the back of Sam's left hand. She wished she could do the same to the one on Sam's heart. "I don't want to hurt you, Sam. I just want to be your friend. Let me see you. All of you."

"I've already bared my soul to you," Sam said miserably. "What's left?"

"Your heart."

Olivia watched Sam's defensive shields slide back into place. "I can't share what isn't mine to give."

CHAPTER SEVEN

Sam woke in a panic. It took her several minutes to realize what was wrong. Last night was the first time in years she hadn't dreamed about Bailey. She had slept fitfully, but her mind had been filled with images from the current expedition not one from her past. Had she finally put Mont Blanc behind her? If so, she had Olivia Bradshaw to thank.

She propped herself up on her elbows and regarded Olivia's sleeping form. Olivia looked so peaceful Sam didn't want to rouse her. From here on out, the climb would be about pain. Experiencing it, accepting it, managing it, overcoming it, or giving in to it. Sam wanted to spare Olivia from that reality for a few more precious moments. But Olivia had signed up for this. She knew what she was in for. She seemed eager—almost too eager—to face the challenge. Was she trying to prove something to herself or someone else?

Sam placed her hand on Olivia's shoulder and gently shook her. "Rise and shine."

Olivia stirred and stretched, her beautiful face drawn into a weary frown. "Is it time?" she asked, shielding her eyes from the glare of Sam's headlamp.

"We've got an hour to clean up and grab something to eat before we head out. I'm taking breakfast orders. What would you like?"

"Steak and eggs, a loaf of French bread, and a pitcher of mimosas would be nice, but I'll settle for whatever you have."

"One MRE coming up."

Olivia crawled out of her sleeping bag. "Dibs on the shower," she said with a mouth-stretching yawn.

Sam laughed despite herself. The joke never got old, no matter how many times she heard it. And she'd heard it plenty. Neither she nor Olivia had seen indoor plumbing in weeks. They wouldn't see any for at least another month. Sam couldn't wait to feel hot water sliding over her skin. For a brief moment, she allowed herself to imagine Olivia's hands doing the same.

She tried to concentrate on something considerably less exciting like deciding which MRE to make for breakfast, but Olivia's suggestion of steak and eggs sounded much more appetizing than any of the selections she had to choose from. Her stomach growled in agreement.

Olivia rolled up her sleeping bag and rummaged through her backpack. She cleaned her face with no-rinse wipes and washed her hair with waterless shampoo. She combed her tangled locks as best she could without a mirror. Then she put on her helmet and buckled it under her chin. She shined her headlamp against the far wall of the tent to test the strength of the beam.

Sam was impressed by Olivia's meticulous preparations. If only she could convince her to be as thoughtful on the mountain. Sometimes she watched Olivia climb with her heart in her throat. Olivia's boundless enthusiasm was refreshing but nerve-wracking, too. Especially when she reminded her of Bailey.

Olivia slowly turned to look at her. Her eyes were clouded with concern. "Is something wrong?"

Sam's mouth went dry. She wanted to voice her concerns, but she didn't know how to put them into words without shaking Olivia's confidence. Out here, there was no room for doubt.

"Are you okay?" Olivia dropped the equipment in her hands and rushed over to her.

Sam nodded. "I'm fine. I just—I wanted to—" She felt rattled. Unsure of herself. When she finally found her footing, she held Olivia's face in her hands and impulsively pressed her lips to hers.

Olivia inhaled sharply. Her body stiffened. Her hands fluttered at her sides as if she didn't know where to place them. They eventually landed on Sam's hips, resting as lightly as butterflies on a flower petal.

Slowly, Olivia's body relaxed. Her lips parted. Sam wanted to explore Olivia's mouth with her tongue. She wanted to undress her. Lay her down on the air mattress and feel her body respond to hers. Fighting to regain control, she broke the kiss before it deepened.

"I just wanted to say thank you."

Olivia swayed, suddenly unsteady on her feet. She tightened her grip on Sam's waist. "You're welcome."

Sam stroked Olivia's cheeks with her thumbs, then turned and walked away. She had a job to do. And her job description didn't include getting Olivia Bradshaw naked.

Olivia spent most of the morning leg lost in thought. She spent it replaying the kiss. She could still feel Sam's warm lips sliding against hers. Feel her muscular hips curving under her fingers.

After Sam rebuffed her advances the night before they began their ascent, Olivia had promised to keep her hands to herself. She had sworn the next move—if it came—would be Sam's. Had Sam made her play or was she reading too much into the situation?

Sometimes a thank-you is just a thank-you.

She tried to remain clinical. If she inserted logic and removed emotion, she'd be less likely to do something she might regret.

Yesterday was an emotional day from beginning to end. She needed contact. So did I. The kiss was just that. A kiss. Not an invitation to fly off to the nearest progressive state and get married.

She ran a gloved hand over her lips.

If it didn't mean anything, why am I counting the minutes until I can do it again?

She gave herself a firm shake to remind herself to stay in the present. If she allowed her mind to wander, she could end up battered and broken at the bottom of a ravine. She could end up like Sanath. She could end up like Bailey.

If worst came to worst, who besides her mother, Chance, and Gigi would mourn her loss? She had a large number of acquaintances, but she could count the number of her friends—real friends—on one hand. As for lovers, the last real relationship she'd had was so long ago it was nothing but a distant memory. In many ways, she had lived a rich, full life. Only now was she beginning to realize how much was missing.

"Okay back there, Doc?" Sam asked.

They'd been climbing for five hours with another three hours to go. Olivia's legs got heavier with each step, her breathing more labored. She was in the best shape of her life, but the eight-hour hike was kicking her ass. Sam looked like she could climb all day. How had she developed such endless reserves? Was she this indefatigable in bed, too?

"I was just wondering if you had received any updates from Rae or the others."

"I was waiting for the sun to come up before I hailed Rae." Sam checked her watch. "It's after nine. I shouldn't be disturbing her beauty sleep if I call her now." She keyed the radio microphone three times in rapid succession, sending quick bursts of static to the base camp receiver. "Hey, Rae, you got your ears on?"

"They're on," Rae said after a moment's pause. "What can I do you for?"

"We got some weather at Camp Two yesterday. How does it look between Three and Four?"

"The satellite imagery I have is about an hour old. Hold on a tick while I see if I can find something more recent. Here we go. I hope you're wearing your long janes. Temps in the upper forties, wind chill in the lower thirties, and about four feet of hard-packed snow are waiting for you."

Olivia examined the clear blue sky. The air temperature was above freezing and there was very little cloud cover between the ground and the harsh beams of the bright sun. If this kept up, it wouldn't be long before the snow on the lower elevations turned to mush.

Hopefully, we'll be safe and warm with our bellies full of food by then. She laughed softly. *Who knew MREs could be so addictive?*

"No snow melt to speak of?" Sam asked.

"Nope. Not yet, anyway, but I wouldn't let my guard down if I were you. A section could decide to let go at any time. Then it's hold your horses and look out below."

"Roger that."

Olivia remembered watching footage of avalanches during one of her high school science classes. She had gasped when she'd seen the raging river of snow take out everything in its path. The destructive power of Mother Nature had taken her breath away. She wasn't eager to witness that power firsthand.

She adjusted her sunglasses. Even though she was wearing polarized lenses, the sun's glare off the pristine snow was nearly blinding. She peered up at the mountain. Wisps of what looked like smoke drifted toward the sky. If they were that close to camp, shouldn't they have made contact with the others by now?

Her cell phone buzzed twice, alerting her she had a message of some kind. She fished the phone out of her pocket and looked at the display. The text message icon glowed brightly on the bottom of the screen. She thumbed over to it. A lengthy message appeared below Gigi's cell phone number.

Almost home. Waiting 2 board flight from Newark 2 Denver. Mob scene @ airport. Someone tipped press 2 R arrival. C's agent working OT. Already scheduled interviews w/all major networks & lined up slew of new endorsements. Will need ur help keeping C's ego in check after commercials air. LOL. Call us when u reach the top. We're rooting for u. Stay safe.

Olivia removed her gloves and held them between her teeth so she could type a quick reply. She was relieved to hear Chance was back on his feet and making the rounds. The guilt she had felt when he had been forced to leave before reaching the summit began to dissipate. Now she could stop worrying about him and concentrate on the task at hand: conquering the mountain that had defeated so many.

She was determined to become Annapurna I's victor, not another of its victims.

❖

Sam was worried. She hadn't been able to reach Pasang on the radio all morning. Her first effort, shortly after her conversation with Rae, might have been too early. With nowhere to go and nothing to do, Pasang, Marie-Eve, and Peter might have been sleeping in. She had waited two hours before trying again. Neither the second nor the third time had proven to be the charm. Now it was nearly noon with still no word. She hadn't voiced her fears, but Jimmy, as usual, seemed to read her mind.

"Maybe the radio batteries died," he said with a shrug after her latest failed attempt. "With me away from home so often, my son has always acted older than his age. I wish it wasn't in the middle of a climb, but he's entitled to be irresponsible every now and then." He gave a half-hearted laugh. "He's probably sitting around having too much fun with people his own age to remember he's being paid to look after them, not party with them."

Sam hoped he was right. She hoped the feeling in her gut was wrong. She hoped Marie-Eve was teaching Pasang how to roll blunts and tell bawdy jokes. She hoped Peter was giving him the kind of attention he didn't often receive in the far reaches of Nepal. She hoped he wasn't, as she suspected, in over his head.

"I asked him to babysit," she said under her breath. "I asked him to keep an eye on things. How hard can that be?" Staring up at the large white flakes that continued to fall from the sky, she answered her own question. "Harder than it looks."

She trained her binoculars toward Camp Three and slowly spun the focus wheel to adjust the magnification. From a distance, the camp looked deserted. The only movement she detected came from the multicolored tents flapping in the wind.

Where was everyone?

Her heart rate quickened when she heard an ominous rumble. The ground shook. She spread her arms and bent her knees to maintain her balance.

Olivia mirrored her stance. "Is it an earthquake?"

"Worse." Sam took a quick look with the binoculars. "It's an avalanche. And it's bearing down fast."

❖

"Tie on!" Sam shouted twice, once in English and once in Nepali.

As Jimmy quickly unspooled a long length of robe, Sam pushed a nearby boulder to test its stability. The jagged rock didn't budge. Olivia judged it to be about six feet tall with a weight of close to twenty tons. Sam shoved her toward the massive stone.

"This will anchor you. Wrap your arms around it and hold on as tight as you can."

Sam's voice shook, a byproduct, Olivia guessed, of the adrenaline coursing through her body. Her own heart galloped in her chest like Secretariat closing in on the finish line at the Belmont. She thought she had prepared herself for the isolation and sense of exposure climbers felt when they reached altitudes normally occupied by low-flying airplanes, but her growing sense of helplessness made her realize she hadn't prepared as well as she thought. This situation was way out of her area of expertise. Panic lurked at the edges of her psyche. The clear head she prided herself on was clouded with apprehension.

The "smoke" she had seen earlier was snow barreling down the mountain. Snow that was now headed straight for them. They had no place to go and nothing to hide behind except a boulder that, if it dislodged, could topple over and crush them or drag them over the edge. If it held, they might have a chance. Emphasis on might. But what about the others? Were Marie-Eve, Peter, and Pasang above the danger zone, or had they been caught up in the maelstrom now roaring toward her?

Sam raced to the other side of the boulder.

"Where are you going?" Tightening her grip on the rock, Olivia craned her neck to follow Sam's movements.

Sam's face filled her vision. Her eyes radiated calm, soothing Olivia's fears.

"Don't worry. I'm not going far." She tied one end of the rope around the boulder and affixed it with a sturdy knot. Then she wrapped three loops around Olivia's waist, took two steps backward, and wrapped three loops around her own body before passing the rest of the rope to Lhakpa, who fed the rope through a bolt bored into the mountain before wrapping it around himself and tossing the rest to Jimmy. Though she and her crew moved in a rush, Sam took time to explain their actions. "Safety in numbers," she said, bracing against the mountainside. "If we tie on, we can stay together."

Together. How could one word inspire such hope?

"Hold on," Sam said. "We're going to be fine."

Whether she meant them or not, Sam said the words with such conviction, Olivia couldn't help but believe her.

The noise filled her ears. The sound of air, water, snow, and debris combining to form a new entity. The sound of a horrible nightmare come to life.

Olivia closed her eyes and braced herself for impact. The snow slammed into the boulder with such force she felt the monolith tilt on its axis.

"Please," she whispered. "Please hold."

Thick clouds of snow powder enveloped her, stinging her skin and filling her lungs. The rapid flow knocked her off her feet. The rope tightened around her waist as Sam, Lhakpa, and Jimmy lost their footing as well. She groaned in pain as the pressure on her ribs mounted. How much could they take before they began to crack?

Lhakpa spoke in Nepali. The words came so fast Olivia couldn't make them out. They sounded like a prayer. When he was done, she offered her own fervent, "Amen."

The flow drifted for another thousand feet before finally coming to a stop. Then, just like that, it was over.

Olivia lay where she had fallen. Her chest heaved as the air began to clear. Her rapid breathing sounded unnaturally loud in the sudden quiet. Sam, Lhakpa, and Jimmy shook snow off their clothes. They looked like forest creatures just waking up after spending a long winter in hibernation. Olivia lay back and laughed, nearly hysterical with relief.

"Don't relax just yet," Sam said. "We have to find the others."

The laughter died in Olivia's throat. What if the others hadn't been as fortunate as they had been? What if they were buried under the snow?

"How do we get back to them?" The well-marked route they had been following was covered by snow. "The path is gone."

Sam pulled her to her feet. "We don't need one."

What was it she had said in the dark?

Climbing was easy for me. It was intuitive. Instinctive. I didn't have to think. I could just see the path I was supposed to take.

"Follow me."

Olivia obediently fell in line. "How much time did you say we had to find them before it would be too late?"

"Fifteen minutes."

Sam's sober expression betrayed her thoughts. They'd never make it in time.

CHAPTER EIGHT

S am flinched when the radio crackled to life.
"Please. Can anyone hear me? Over."
Olivia gripped her arm. "That's Peter's voice. They're alive."
At least one of them is.
"I read you, Peter," Sam said. "What's your status?"
"Sam, if you're out there, please respond. Over."
"He's so panicked he's forgetting to release the microphone when he's finished talking," Olivia said.
Sam kept trying to respond to Peter's calls even though her efforts appeared to be in vain. "Peter, I read you. What's your status? I repeat. What's your status? Over."
Peter cursed in German. "I think the radio's broken, but I'm going to keep talking because I don't know what else to do. Pasang, Marie-Eve, and I were separated when the avalanche swept through. Pasang and I dug ourselves out, but we can't find Marie-Eve. We've both been looking for twenty minutes now. I had to stop for a while to catch my breath. Pasang seems to be okay despite a nasty gash on his head. He's probing the snow now. Wait. I think he may have found something. He's holding up a glove. Pasang, what is it? Did you find—"
The transmission abruptly ended.
"Shit." Sam shoved the radio into Olivia's hands. "Keep trying to reach out to him. Try to find out what's going on."
She fished the transceiver out of her pocket as she quickened her pace. If Marie-Eve's beacon was working properly, she should be able to home in on the signal from up to eighty meters away. She

switched the unit to receive mode and stared at the digital display, which was supposed to provide visual indication of the direction and distance to a buried victim. Camp Three was about a hundred meters away, close enough for her to see the flags marking the campsite, but not close enough for the transceiver to get a signal.

"I'm not getting anything. What about you?"

Olivia shook her head. She keyed the microphone again. "Peter, come in."

"There they are," Jimmy said.

Sam looked in the direction he was pointing. She spotted Pasang and Peter frantically pawing at the snow.

Even if a snow pack consisted of loose powder as this one had, avalanche debris refroze as soon as the snow stopped moving. The debris was too dense to be manipulated by hand.

"Shovels. They need shovels."

Jimmy and Lhakpa grabbed shovels and ran up the mountain. Sam followed closely behind, her eyes on the transceiver's display. The beacon beeped. A fuzzy image appeared on the screen.

"I've got a signal." Jimmy and Lhakpa sprinted faster, their boots crunching on the tightly compressed snow. "Tell them they're in the wrong spot. She's five meters to the left of their location."

Olivia raised the radio transmitter to her mouth and relayed the information.

Pasang and Peter stopped digging and crawled to the new location. Pasang poked a collapsible aluminum probe into the snow. The probe sank deep into the snow again and again. Sam was tempted to take the probe from him and do the search herself, but she didn't want to embarrass Pasang in front of the others. Confidence, once lost, was difficult to regain.

Her patience was rewarded several long minutes later when she heard the thud of the probe making contact with something soft.

Pasang's face lit up. "Here," he said in Nepali. "She's right here."

Jimmy rested a hand on his shoulder. "How deep?"

Pasang swiped at the blood running down his face. Droplets spilled on the snow like discarded Valentine's Day candies. "One meter. Maybe two."

Jimmy and Lhakpa marked off a six-foot by three-foot rectangle and began to dig.

As Pasang and Peter struggled to catch their breath, Olivia pulled out her medical bag and examined them both. Peter had a nosebleed brought on by altitude and exertion. Blood poured out of both nostrils and pooled in his scraggly beard. Olivia packed cotton in his nose to staunch the flow and handed him a bottle of Gatorade to replenish his electrolytes. He gripped the bottle in one hand, Marie-Eve's glove in the other. His eyes were wide with shock.

Olivia put on a fresh pair of latex gloves before she turned to Pasang. Holding his dark hair away from his forehead, she squirted saline on the cut on his scalp. The wound bled profusely as all head lacerations were wont to do, but from Sam's vantage point, it didn't appear to be very deep. Olivia covered the cut with a wad of gauze and a pair of butterfly bandages.

Sam loved watching Olivia work. She discharged her duties with clinical precision balanced by tender concern. No movements were wasted, but her touch was gentle, judging from Peter's and Pasang's reactions to her ministrations.

"Thank you, Dr. Bradshaw," Pasang said.

Both he and Peter looked like they wanted to resume digging, but they wisely stayed put. If they pushed themselves any further, Sam feared they might collapse.

Excavating an avalanche victim took time. So much time that many victims suffocated before they could be reached. As Jimmy and Lhakpa dug through the snow, Sam focused on the transceiver in her hands. She stared at the display, desperate to see signs of life.

"Come on, kid. Give me something besides a hard time."

By her calculations, Marie-Eve had been buried under the snow for nearly thirty minutes—twice as long as the average survivor. Despite the overwhelming odds, Sam held out hope. Marie-Eve was a hockey player. She trained and competed in frigid temperatures all the time. If anyone could make it through this, she could.

Sam shouted encouragement to Jimmy and Lhakpa, who seemed to be slowing down. Perspiration dripped from their faces. Soaked their clothes. "Keep going. You're almost there."

Jimmy tossed his shovel aside and reached for a metal scoop. That meant he was getting close.

"We've got her."

Lhakpa freed Marie-Eve's legs just before Jimmy uncovered her upper body. Marie-Eve was curled into the fetal position, her hands cupped around her mouth. Her eyes were closed, her skin blue. Her features, normally so vibrant and alive, were deathly still. She wasn't breathing.

"Doc?"

Sam turned to Olivia, who immediately lowered herself into the hole. Olivia pressed two fingers against the side of Marie-Eve's neck and held them there. "I've got a pulse. It's weak and thready, but it's there. Does anyone have a mirror?"

"How about this?" Sam held up her compass. "Will this work?"

"It's worth a shot." Olivia flipped open the nickel-plated lid and held the compass face under Marie-Eve's nose. A few seconds later, condensation formed on the glass.

"Yes." Sam clenched her fists as Peter whooped in celebration.

Olivia ran her hands over Marie-Eve's body, checking for broken bones. "Okay," she said at last, "let's get her out of here."

Jimmy and Lhakpa lifted Marie-Eve's limp body out of the hole.

"We've got to get her warm and dry," Sam said. "Which one's her tent?"

"This one," Peter said, leading the way.

Held in place by snow anchors and ice axes, the tents had managed to remain intact during the avalanche's onslaught. Jimmy and Lhakpa carried Marie-Eve inside the one Peter indicated.

"Why isn't she waking up?" he asked after they lay her down.

Olivia lifted Marie-Eve's eyelids with her thumbs. Marie-Eve's pupils were as small as pinpoints. "She's in shock. Her brain is shutting her body down until it's had enough time to recover."

"How long will that take?"

"That's up to her. The sooner we get her temperature up, the less time it should take."

Olivia pulled off Marie-Eve's boots and socks. Sam caught her eye. "Are you thinking what I'm thinking?"

Olivia nodded once. "Body heat."

Peter wrung his hands. He reminded Sam of an anxious expectant father. "I'll be outside. You'll let me know if her condition changes?"

"Of course."

He ducked out of the tent and closed the flap behind him.

While Olivia peeled off Marie-Eve's wet clothes, Sam unrolled two sleeping bags and zipped them together. She spread the newly formed double bag on the floor of the tent. After she helped Olivia slip Marie-Eve's naked body inside, she began to remove her own clothes. "Fore or aft?"

"Aft. I need to be able to take her vital signs—and yours, if need be. Our temps are going to dip while we try to raise hers."

You don't have to worry about me, Doc. Thanks to you, I'm generating enough heat right now to warm a small country.

Sam had to force herself not to watch Olivia undress.

What would happen if I did? One quick peek could fuel my fantasies for years to come. She closed her eyes until she regained her resolve. *No. This isn't the time or the place.*

Olivia evidently wasn't harboring such qualms. Sam could feel Olivia's eyes on her. As she pulled off her thermal underwear, she turned an unnecessary pirouette to give Olivia a better view of the phoenix tattooed on her back. The legendary creature stretched from her hips to her shoulders. She had been drawn to the sketch pinned to the artist's wall. The red and orange bird didn't seem born of fire but made from it.

"Beautiful," Olivia whispered. She stammered when Sam turned to face her. Did her fingers itch to trace the intricate design on her skin? Did her tongue long to douse the flames? "The tattoo, I mean. Did you get it done here?"

"No. I got it in Alaska after I summited Mt. McKinley. The tat took almost as long as the climb."

"My congratulations to the artist. Wonderful work. Then again, he had a wonderful canvas to work with."

Olivia licked her lips. Sam's clit grew rigid. Her nipples, already puckered from the cold, felt like they could cut glass.

Her body wasn't something she worked to maintain. It was something she maintained through work. She wasn't immune to the effect she had on others, but it had been years since someone had a similar effect on her. Was Olivia Bradshaw the one who had changed that—or was the change coming from within? Either way, she didn't have time to find out.

Grateful Marie-Eve would act as a barrier between her and Olivia, Sam slipped inside the sleeping bag. They had positioned Marie-Eve on her side. Sam pressed her back against Marie-Eve's front. Olivia pressed her front to her back.

Sam began to shiver. "Her skin feels like ice." When Olivia began to move, Sam turned to see what she was doing. "What's that?" she asked as Olivia rubbed something that looked like a miniature electric razor over Marie-Eve's forehead.

"A temporal artery thermometer. It's non-invasive, which reassures nervous patients, and uses infrared technology to take a thousand readings per second in order to provide the most accurate results."

"What else do you have in your bag of tricks?"

Olivia winked. "You'd be surprised." The thermometer beeped softly. The bright red LED display provided a stark contrast to the dark expression on Olivia's face. "Her core temp's only ninety-three degrees."

"Then I guess we're going to be here a while." Sam snuggled closer. She stuck her tongue between her teeth to keep them from chattering. "Care to guess the first thing she's going to say when she wakes up?"

Olivia smoothed Marie-Eve's damp curls. "Something humorous, I'm sure. Or what passes for humor in that twisted mind of hers."

Sam laughed, remembering some of the endless stream of witticisms that had fallen from Marie-Eve's lips over the past few weeks. She had found the jokes annoying at the time, but she would give anything to hear Marie-Eve tell another one. "She is going to wake up, isn't she?"

"Yes, she is. And when she does, I get to tell her this was your idea."

Sam didn't have to turn around to picture the smile on Olivia's face. "My idea? You threw out the words 'body heat' before I did."

"Yet you still managed to get undressed first."

"I didn't know we were running a race."

"If we were, I would have come in a distant second. I had no idea you were such an exhibitionist. With a body like yours, though, I can't blame you for wanting to show it off."

Sam felt a blush rapidly work its way from the tips of her toes to the top of her head. The body Olivia had just complimented was on fire.

Marie-Eve stirred but didn't open her eyes. "I love when women fight over me," she said.

Startled, Sam sucked in her breath. "Is she coming around?"

Olivia took another temperature reading. This time the display read ninety-four. "Not yet, but we're headed in the right direction."

Olivia draped her arm across Marie-Eve's waist. Her hand rested on Sam's hip. Sam covered the hand with her own.

"Yes, I think we are."

CHAPTER NINE

Marie-Eve sighed as Olivia subjected her to yet another examination. "Doc, I'm fine."

"Why don't you let me be the judge of that?"

Marie-Eve had regained consciousness the morning after Jimmy and Lhakpa dug her out of the snow. She had tried to get up and move around as soon as she came to, but Olivia had insisted she remain on bed rest for forty-eight hours while she checked her for physical and/or neurological impairment. The only visible sign of damage was a slight case of frostbite on her right hand, which had been left unprotected after the force of the avalanche ripped off the glove Pasang had found several feet from her body. The gangrene Olivia dreaded had not set in, however. Marie-Eve's fingertips, which had been bright red for the better part of three days, now bore a healthy pink pallor.

The summit party had been at Camp Three for nearly four days, giving the two other expedition teams on the mountain ample time to catch and pass them. Olivia had watched the groups from Ecuador and Japan sweep past with a hint of ambivalence. Though she wanted hers to be the first of the three teams to reach the summit, she wasn't willing to put her team members' lives in danger in order to satisfy her competitive urges.

Slow and steady wins the race, she reminded herself.

Their original itinerary had called for a two-night stay at Camp Three. The extra downtime had put the trek behind schedule. Olivia felt the clock ticking, but she wanted to make sure Marie-

Eve sufficiently recovered from her ordeal before she gave the okay to continue the ascent. She couldn't risk delaying their departure much longer, though, or they might burn through their initial round of supplies before they made it back to base camp.

"Follow my finger." Marie-Eve's eyes remained focused and clear as they tracked Olivia's index finger through the air. "Good. Now squeeze my hands. Ow! I said squeeze them, not break them."

"Sorry, Doc." Despite the apology, Marie-Eve seemed pleased by her show of strength.

"Let's check your balance. Stand up straight, lean your head back, and spread your arms. Excellent. Now touch your left index finger to the tip of your nose."

"Are you testing my balance or my sobriety?" Marie-Eve asked with a skeptical cock of her head.

"Both. I know you've had pot recently. When was the last time you had alcohol?"

"Longer than I care to remember. I'm dying for a beer. At this point, I don't care if it tastes like yak piss as long as it's fermented and comes in a bottle."

"When we get back to base camp, the first round's on me."

"It's a deal." Marie-Eve touched her left index finger, then her right to the tip of her nose. "Do I pass?" She arched her eyebrows expectantly.

"Yes," Olivia said, "but I'm going to give you the same lecture I gave Chance. You know your body better than I do. If something doesn't feel right—"

"Don't keep it to myself. I got it, Doc. Can we go now?" She rubbed her palms together in youthful exuberance. "I want to tackle that ice ridge."

Olivia tried to think of a reason to say no. If her research was correct, the first part of the climb had been easy compared to what was to come. Even though Marie-Eve had passed all her tests, was she truly prepared to tackle the most physically taxing part of the ascent? She said she was. Olivia decided to take her word for it, but she planned to keep her on a short leash just in case.

"Don't make me regret trusting you."

"Never. One more thing." Marie-Eve's playful grin turned roguish. "Waking up between you and Sam has convinced me to amend my views on sleeping with older women. Whenever you two hard bodies are ready to make another sandwich out of me, just say the word, okay? I'll gladly be your filling any time."

Olivia's lingering doubts disappeared. Marie-Eve was back to her old self.

Marie-Eve strutted toward Sam and surprised her with a cheeky swat on her butt, then narrowly avoided being rewarded with a punch in the mouth in return. They sparred for a few seconds, feinting and jabbing like a pair of pugilists in training.

Olivia watched the playful interaction between them. Not long ago, they were butting heads at every turn. Now they were practically bosom buddies.

Sharing body heat tends to promote friendship.

She closed her eyes, remembering the sight of Sam's body in all its sculpted perfection. The chiseled legs. The toned arms. The rippled abs. The tight breasts. And that amazing tattoo. She could still see the phoenix. Mouth open, wings spread as if preparing to take flight.

She remembered the feel of Sam's firm hip beneath her hand. The warmth of Sam's fingers laced through hers. For a moment, she had forgotten the reason they were there. She had forgotten about the climb. She had forgotten about the avalanche. She had forgotten about the other disasters—natural and man-made—that had befallen them on the way. She had forgotten everything except the sound of Sam's breathing. The softness of her skin. The taste of her kiss.

She opened her eyes before her imagination ran wild. She didn't have time for romance, real or imagined.

Her pleasant memories of Sam's body were tempered by the pain in her own. Though she had survived the avalanche, she had not come through it unscathed. Purple bruises dotted her sides. Two bright red marks circled her waist where the rope had bitten through her clothes. She rubbed her sore ribs. Breathing was uncomfortable. Coughing was excruciating. Taking a deep breath was impossible. If she couldn't keep her lungs clear, she could become susceptible to a bronchial infection, a malady that often proved debilitating at sea level, let alone at altitude.

She popped a couple ibuprofen to dull the pain. She'd be damned if she'd allow a few sore ribs to keep her from accomplishing her goal of reaching the summit.

Physician, heal thyself.

❖

Sam checked and re-checked the equipment. She inspected the bindings on the harnesses, examined the ropes for frays, and looked for defects in the carabiners and ascenders. Everything passed muster. If something went wrong today, human, not equipment failure would be to blame.

They had made it to the ice ridge. For the first time, the climbers would work in two-person teams instead of as individuals. The ridge's incline was steep, though not steep enough for the climbers to be tied together. Instead, they would ascend side-by-side, clinging to ropes set three feet apart.

Chance and Gigi's departure had necessitated changes to her initial pairings. She and Lhakpa would keep their original partners, but Jimmy and Pasang would alternately pair with Peter. Pasang would take lead on the ice ridge, a strenuous but manageable fourteen hundred foot climb. Jimmy would ascend the ridge solo, checking the ice for faults and inspecting the fixed ropes the others would later clip on to. When they reached the far trickier ice wall in a few days, Jimmy would take lead and Pasang would remain in camp until they descended to base camp to rest for the summit push.

In theory, the pairings seemed solid. The only team that concerned her was Lhakpa and Marie-Eve. Each member of the other pairs had established relationships with their partners. Formed trust. Marie-Eve hadn't interacted with anyone except her fellow team members, none of whom were experienced enough with ice climbing to lead her up the ridge.

Lhakpa helped save her life. Surely, that must count for something.

Peter wandered over as she laid out the equipment. Though he had been nearly manic the first week, he had been relatively subdued since Marie-Eve's accident. Sam regretted the circumstances that brought about Peter's personality change but liked the end result.

"May I talk to you?" he asked. When she nodded her assent, he knelt next to her in the snow. "I just wanted to thank you for everything you've done for us on this trip."

"No need to thank me. I'm just doing my job."

"That's the part I can't figure out. Why would someone who's experienced the tragedy you have climb mountains for a living?"

"What do you mean?"

Alarm bells went off in Sam's head. Peter must have heard them because he couldn't meet her eye. He drew tracks in the snow with his fingers. "Pasang told us about, you know, Mont Blanc."

Sam had told Rae and Jimmy about Mont Blanc years ago. Rae, as far as she knew, hadn't repeated her story to anyone. Jimmy had evidently told Pasang, who hadn't been able to keep the tale to himself.

Peter flicked melting snow off his gloves. "Marie-Eve, Pasang, and I have gotten pretty close during this trip. While you and the others were down at Camp One, the three of us didn't have anything else to do but talk. Pasang told us about...everything you've been through. He told us in strictest confidence and made it quite clear the story was not to be repeated. I won't mention it on my vlog or anywhere else for that matter. Your secret's safe with me, Sam." He extended his hand. "Thank you for saving Marie-Eve. And please accept my condolences. For Sanath and for Bailey."

A lump formed in Sam's throat. She tried to swallow it down. Each day of this trip, she felt more accepting of her past. More comfortable with her present. Would she eventually come to terms with both? The prospect, which she once thought unreachable, now seemed attainable.

❖

Jimmy climbed the ridge first. Olivia envied his economy of motion. His smooth movements made a difficult task look uncomplicated. Lhakpa and Marie-Eve followed, each clipping on to one of the pair of ropes draped across the steep incline. Olivia watched their progress with trepidation. Less than a week ago, Marie-Eve was virtually at death's door. Now she was resuming her ascent of one of the world's deadliest mountains. Would she make it to the top of the ice ridge or run out of steam along the way? Seemingly mindful of Marie-Eve's recent travails, Lhakpa set a nice, easy pace. Marie-Eve matched his tempo with little effort. When she and Lhakpa climbed off the ridge and joined Jimmy in Camp Four, Olivia could hear her jubilation even from afar.

"Pasang. Peter. You're up next." Sam made sure their crampons and harnesses were secure before she sent them on their way.

Pasang and Peter worked well together. Pasang set the pace and Peter matched his rhythm. It was almost like watching them make love.

As Pasang and Peter continued to climb, Olivia looked over at Sam. Her expression was mixed with equal parts pride and apprehension.

What must have been going through her mind? After the tragedy in Mont Blanc, the unease she felt each time she watched relative novices climb a sheet of ice must be overwhelming. She appeared outwardly calm, but Olivia could sense her inner turmoil. Sam chewed her lip as she cast anxious glances at Pasang's and Peter's departing forms. She adjusted and readjusted the fit of her helmet. Subtle but obvious signs of the pressure she was placing on herself. Pressure Olivia felt as well. Until they reached the rock bands above the ice wall, they would be under constant threat of an avalanche. One bitch slap from Mother Nature was enough.

"Nervous?" Sam asked.

"I was hoping it didn't show." Olivia tried to laugh. Even to her own ears, her attempt sounded hollow and forced.

"Remind me not to take you to Vegas any time soon, Doc. You need to work on your poker face."

Whether seriously or in jest, this was the first time Sam had mentioned continuing their acquaintance after the climb ended. Did

Sam want to see her again or was she simply trying to keep her spirits up before they took on the ice ridge?

Olivia looked up at the jagged sheet of ice.

Better to ask her after the leg than before.

"Ready?" Sam tugged on the long nylon ropes.

"As ready as I'll ever be."

Sam clamped her ascender, also known as a jumar, to one of the ropes and slid it up the line. After she pulled herself up with the jumar, she dug the toe of her right boot into the ice. She followed suit with her left. She repeated the process again and again, climbing the steep slope a few feet at a time. On a parallel line, Olivia mirrored her movements. Whenever Sam began to pull ahead, she slowed to allow Olivia to catch up to her. Each time Olivia drew even, Sam offered her encouragement.

"Good job. Way to go. We'll be in camp in no time."

Halfway into the climb, Olivia began to wonder if Sam's idea of "in no time" was radically different from hers. Using her crampons like emergency brakes, she tried not to slide down the ice as she paused to catch her breath.

Even though the ridge was cold to the touch, its frozen surface collected energy like a solar panel. The UV rays reflecting off the ice made Olivia feel as if she were roasting inside a microwave. The ibuprofen had barely taken the edge off the ache in her ribs, multiplying the discomfort of the climb.

Many mountaineers embraced climbing not for the thrill of reaching the summit but for the purifying pain they felt on the way.

If this trip is supposed to be cleansing, I should be as pure as a bar of Ivory soap by the time it's over.

A sharp twinge in her side nearly buckled her knees.

She didn't think her ribs were broken, but at least one was definitely cracked. She was willing to bet her license on it.

She dragged her forearm across her sweat-drenched forehead. She needed something to distract her from the pain—and the fact that she was precariously perched on a slippery, ice-covered slope some twenty thousand feet above the ground.

"Sex on the Beach, an Old-Fashioned, or a dirty martini?" she asked when she pulled even with Sam.

Sam looked at her as if she just sprouted a second head. "Excuse me?"

"Something new school, something old school, or a bit of both. Which do you prefer?"

"I don't do umbrella drinks. I'm a Gorkha kind of girl."

The muscles in Olivia's legs trembled with effort even as she felt the tension leave her shoulders. "I don't think that was an option."

Sam flashed a ghost of a smile. "If you want to get inside my head, Doc, you need to broaden your horizons."

With two long strides and a powerful pull on her ascender, Sam advanced up the mountain. Olivia chased after her. After fifteen minutes of steady climbing, Sam slowed to let her catch up. Olivia quickly closed the gap. If their previous encounter was any indication, she would be allowed to ask only one question before Sam moved on. She needed to make it a good one.

"Boxers, briefs, or granny panties?"

Sam laughed so loud the sound echoed off the ridge. "Granny panties."

"Nope. Try again. I distinctly remember seeing you step out of a pair of bikini briefs a few days ago."

Sam's smile grew. "Then why ask a question you already know the answer to?"

In a flash, she was gone again, and Olivia was once more forced to pursue her. The extra carabiners she carried crisscrossed her chest like bandoliers, making her feel like a long-lost soldier from the Mexican Revolution. The metal loops tinkled like wind chimes as she raced after Sam.

"Truth or Dare, Scrabble, or Monopoly?"

"I don't play games."

Sam's eyes bore into hers. Olivia grabbed the metaphorical wheel before the conversation fishtailed into more serious subjects. "Not even Sudoku?"

"Not even. Unless there's something else you want to ask me, I'm going to get back to climbing now."

Olivia watched Sam's tight ass rise above her, the most tantalizing carrot on a stick she had ever seen. "Don't worry. I'll think of something."

Sam looked back at her and grinned. "I'm sure you will."

"Classic car, Harley, or hybrid?" Olivia asked during the next round of questions.

"That's an easy one. A jet black nineteen sixty-five Mustang convertible with red leather seats, a white hardtop, seventeen-inch tires, and all the original accessories."

Olivia could see herself riding down the highway with the top down and vintage tunes blasting. The wind in her hair, the sun on her face, and Sam's arm across her shoulders. She was amazed how quickly the images came to mind and how right they seemed.

She thought she and Sam were well on their way to becoming friends, but she couldn't decide if she wanted friendship to be the final destination or simply the starting point on an even greater journey.

"Bruce Springsteen, the Beatles, or the Rolling Stones?"

"Fleetwood Mac before they started experimenting with the lineup. Give me Stevie Nicks's rasp and Christine McVie's smoke and I'm all yours."

Olivia made a mental note to update the playlist on her iPod.

"We're running out of real estate, Doc. You'd better hurry if you want to get to the good stuff."

Olivia looked up. Roughly sixty feet separated them from the top of the ridge. She had time for one more question, two at the most. She had learned more about Sam in the past seven hundred feet than she had in the previous twenty thousand. Why did today's leg have to be so short?

"Happily ever after or to be continued?"

"In the real world, there's no such thing as happily ever after." Sam's eyes lost some of their previous luster. "But if you're talking about a book or a movie, I hate plunking down twenty bucks and walking away pissed at the end. Give me the sappy finish every time."

"I never pictured you as a hopeless romantic."

"I'm not. I'm just hopeless."

"So you say. I'm not planning on giving up on you just yet."

Olivia removed one glove and brushed her fingers across Sam's cheek. She sensed such a dichotomy in Sam. Physically powerful yet emotionally vulnerable. The contrast tugged at her heart.

She traced the line of Sam's strong jaw with the back of her hand. She looked into her eyes, daring her to pull away. Sam moved closer. She leaned against Olivia's hand, nuzzling her cheek against her palm like a kitten begging to be stroked.

"One last question." Olivia moved her hand to the nape of Sam's neck. She wove her fingers through the short locks that peeked out of the back of Sam's helmet. "Top or bottom?"

Marie-Eve's voice broke the spell. "Are you two going to hang out making goo-goo eyes at each other all day," she said, leaning out over the ridge, "or are you planning on joining the rest of us sometime soon?"

Sam chuckled as she moved away. "Tell me again why we wanted her to wake up."

Olivia flexed her fingers as she pulled her glove over her hand. "It's not too late to knock her out again. If you hold her down, I'll do the honors."

"You got it, Doc," Sam said with a wink that made Olivia's stomach turn somersaults. "See you at the top."

Sam pulled herself over the edge of the ridge and unclipped from the rope. As soon as she slipped off her harness and jumar, Jimmy gathered the discarded equipment and ferried it to the supply tent.

She took a long look at each of the other climbers. None seemed the worse for wear. Marie-Eve was acting as cameraperson while Peter interviewed Pasang for his latest vlog. Jimmy and Lhakpa stood on the sidelines, trying to keep their laughter at bay while Pasang had his fifteen minutes of fame.

Sam turned to make sure Olivia finished strong. She kneeled on the edge of the ridge, ready to give Olivia a hand up as soon as her head appeared at the top of the slope.

"Almost there. Not much farther now."

Olivia was ten feet from the top. Five. In a few more minutes, she would be on solid ground and Sam could breathe easy for a few days. They all could.

Olivia pulled herself hand-over-hand. The rope scraped against the rocks. How long had the faded line been in place? Five years? Ten? How many climbers had used it to aid their ascent? More than Sam could count.

She held out her hand. Olivia reached to take it. Too late, Sam heard the rope's strands start to give way. Too late, she saw the rope begin to shear. Just like with Bailey, she was too late.

The rope broke.

Olivia cried out as she plummeted down the embankment. Sam made a desperate lunge for her hand. Just like with Bailey, Olivia's fingers were just out of reach.

Olivia slid inexorably down the ridge, her crampons slowing but not arresting her descent. The metal spikes screamed as they gouged deep grooves in the ice.

"Olivia!" Sam called after her.

"Doc?" Marie-Eve said. Interview forgotten, she, Pasang, and Peter peered over the edge of the ridge. "Doc!"

Panic rose like a swollen river in Sam's gut, threatening to wash her away.

Olivia's gloved hands slid over the ice, desperately seeking purchase. Finally, fifty feet down, she managed to grab the remaining rope. The nylon line pulled taut as her body jerked to a stop. She held on to the rope with one hand as her momentum sent her crashing into the mountain. With a grunt of effort, she swung the right side of her body around and grasped the rope with her second hand. She wrapped her feet around a bulky knot and held on like a PE student stuck in the middle of a rope climb in the high school gym.

Sam lay on her belly. She wanted to rappel down to her, but in the time it would take to prepare the equipment, Olivia might run out of arm strength. She cupped her hands around her mouth. "Clip onto the rope," she called out. "Use your jumar."

Olivia unlocked her ascender, freed it from the remnants of the severed line dangling from her waist, and attached it to the remaining fixed rope. Then she slowly made her way back up the incline.

Sam didn't take any chances this time. As soon as Olivia neared the top of the ridge, she grabbed her by her shoulders and hauled her over the edge.

"Are you all right?"

Olivia lay on her back, her chest heaving. Her eyes wide. She didn't respond to Sam's question. Was she in shock or had she sustained some kind of head injury that prevented her from speaking?

Trying to rein in an all-too-familiar sense of panic, Sam reached for the radio. "I'll hail BC and get Dr. Curtis on the horn."

"No, don't do that." Olivia slowly sat up. "I'm okay."

"Are you sure?" Sam carefully helped her to her feet as Marie-Eve and Peter rushed to her side.

"I'm fine, Sam. Really."

Olivia flashed a brilliant smile. She seemed too cool, too composed, considering what had just happened. Either she had nerves of steel or she was trying to convince everyone she wasn't as frightened as Sam knew she had to be.

Sam wanted to offer her words of comfort, but when she looked at her, she saw Bailey's face staring back at her. She quickly turned away from the painful apparition.

"You gave us all quite a scare," Peter said.

"Not intentionally, I assure you." Olivia laughed shakily, giving Sam a hint of the inner turmoil lurking beneath her placid surface.

"What happened down there, Doc?" Marie-Eve asked.

"I wish I knew. I was almost done when the rope just...broke."

Olivia waved her hands like a magician who had just made her sequin-clad assistant disappear. Sam's self-confidence disappeared with it. Was the accident her fault? Had she, distracted by her conversation with Olivia, made what had very nearly amounted to a fatal error? She had lost focus during a climb once before and it had cost her dearly.

Over breakfast the morning they set out to climb Mont Blanc, Bailey had asked her how she felt about marriage and children. Before that moment, Sam had never considered the possibility. After Bailey posed the question, settling down and starting a family was all she could think about. She had spent the rest of the morning imagining herself walking with Bailey down a rose-covered aisle. Rubbing Bailey's steadily swelling belly and bickering with her as they perused a book of baby names. She had pictured it all— first steps, first day of school, high school graduation, college commencement. Birthdays, anniversaries, family gatherings. And through it all, through good times and bad, there she and Bailey would be. Looking on proudly. Laughing through their tears. Then, in a matter of hours, the dream had become a nightmare.

"I inspected the rope myself," Jimmy said defensively. "It was intact."

"No one's questioning you, Jimmy," Sam said, even as she continued to question herself.

Eventually, everyone drifted back to camp. Pasang hung his head after his offer of food wasn't met with a great deal of enthusiasm.

"This happened because of me," he said.

"The rope was intact," Sam said. "Jimmy inspected it today. So did I the last time we took this route."

But that was a year ago. She should have inspected it today. She trusted Jimmy—she was confident in his work—but she should have checked behind him. If she had, she wouldn't be spending the rest of the climb wracked with doubt. Neither would Jimmy.

"Why are you blaming yourself?" Sam asked.

Pasang jerked a thumb in Peter's direction. "I tried to tell him jiggy-jiggy on the mountain bring very bad luck."

Peter's face reddened. "You didn't have any complaints when you got what *you* wanted."

He stalked off. Pasang followed suit, heading in the opposite direction.

"Lovers' tiff," Marie-Eve said with a shrug. "I'll see if I can help them kiss and make up."

Sam regarded Olivia as she stared off into the distance. Though Olivia claimed to be unaffected by her accident, Sam could see the truth behind the lie. A few hours ago, Olivia had seemed larger than life. Now she was noticeably smaller. Diminished. Sam wanted to hold her and take away her doubts, but first she had to resolve her own.

She wished she could turn back the clock to prevent today from happening. She would gladly lose the tender moment she and Olivia had shared during the climb in order to prevent the terrifying one that had soon followed.

"Are you sure you're all right?" she asked.

"I'm sure," Olivia said with a smile that was becoming less and less convincing. "I'm going to check on Peter and Pasang."

She looked anxious to get away. Sam knew from experience the last thing Olivia needed right now was to be alone, but Sam let her go. She had to. She needed to put some much-needed distance between them before someone ended up with something much more serious than a broken heart.

As Jimmy and Lhakpa began the laborious task of replacing the broken lengths of rope, Sam mentally retraced her actions over the past twenty-four hours to see if she had deviated in any way from her usual routine during this leg of the climb. The only change was the addition of the impromptu round of Q&A Olivia had subjected her to during their dual climb up the ice ridge.

She had loved hearing Olivia's questions and trying to imagine what Olivia would come up with next. She had been amused by Olivia's quirky sense of humor and fascinated by the way her mind worked. Perhaps too fascinated. If she had been thinking clearly, she would have noticed the frayed rope. She would have been able to get to Olivia before she began her slide. She would have done her job.

She shouldn't have allowed herself to get so close. She had stopped seeing Olivia as a client and started to think of her as something more. Now she had to pull back before it was too late. For everyone.

CHAPTER TEN

In Camp Six, Olivia and the rest of the team used their axes to break off shards of ice Pasang would melt to make fresh water. She placed the latest batch of ice she had collected in a plastic garbage bag, then sat with her elbows on her knees as she tried to slow her racing heart. Ignoring the pain in her ribs, she breathed deeply to allow the oxygen from her portable tank to fill her lungs.

They were nearly a month into the ascent. Twenty-four thousand feet up. A little more than twenty-five hundred feet from the summit. Tomorrow, instead of continuing to climb, they would begin to descend. They would spend three glorious days at base camp resting their weary bodies and minds for the final push to the top. She couldn't wait to have a shower and collapse into a warm bed, even if the bed in question was a thirty-year-old cot that had seen better days.

Her last three meals had consisted of hot tea and crackers, the only solid food she was able to keep down as she battled the unrelenting nausea brought on by the plummeting oxygen levels. Her energy was at an all-time low. She didn't have much of an appetite, but her thirst was insatiable. She took in nearly a gallon of fluids a day as she fought to remain hydrated in the thin, dry air.

She repositioned the oxygen mask over her nose and mouth. The gas wasn't flowing as freely as it had a few minutes earlier. She checked the gauge. The canister was nearly empty. She would need a fresh one before she went to bed. She hated sleeping with the mask on, but she hated waking up gasping for breath even more. She was counting the minutes to tomorrow's descent. When they returned to this spot after a week of breathing the oxygen richer air at base camp, the climb wouldn't prove nearly as taxing as it had the first time around. The weeks of acclimatizing would finally pay off. She hoped.

She pushed herself to her feet and slowly made her way to the mess tent. She added her garbage bag to the growing pile and lifted her oxygen mask long enough to ask, "Do you need more?" She was amazed how easily Nepali came to her now. In a few more weeks, she might be as fluent as a native speaker.

Pasang looked inside the garbage bag and shook his head. "When I add this to what the others harvest, we should have about sixteen liters." He poured freshly melted ice into a canteen. "That's more than enough to get us back to BC."

"Do you need help rationing it out?"

"No, Dr. Bradshaw. I—*We* have it under control." He grinned as his eyes flicked over her shoulder.

She turned to follow his line of sight. Peter stood in the mouth of the tent.

Olivia smiled to herself. *Looks like Marie-Eve is a more skilled negotiator than I gave her credit for. I might have to ask for her help the next time I'm in a bind. Which could be any second now.*

Sam approached the tent, a bulging plastic bag in her arms. Parts of the bag were in tatters, sliced by long shards of ice.

Olivia held the tent flap open as Sam ducked inside. Sam didn't look at her as she brushed past. That was nothing new. Sam had been studiously avoiding her. Olivia wasn't surprised Sam was giving her the cold shoulder. The incident on the ice ridge had probably reminded Sam of Bailey's accident on Mont Blanc. Olivia had tried to downplay her fall in order to prevent Sam from making the inevitable comparison, but those moments of sheer terror weighed heavily on her mind.

She had never felt so close to dying. So completely out of control. She had come face-to-face with her own mortality, the boogeyman she had been running from since she was eleven years old.

She had felt as helpless on the ridge as she had the day she had discovered her father's lifeless body. Only this time it had been worse. Because this time, she'd thought she was prepared. She couldn't have been more wrong.

She had planned for everything Mother Nature had to offer—rain, snow, ice, good weather, and bad—but she hadn't accounted for what the universe had in store. Was karma, fate, or sheer bad luck to blame?

She had been in a fog since that day on the ridge. Thankfully, no one seemed to have noticed. Because of the effects of the high altitude, none of them were at their mental or physical best. But Olivia didn't know how much longer she could keep up the charade. Her emotions were so close to the surface she knew it was only a matter of time before they broke free. When they did, she didn't know if she would be able to regain control of them.

Sam relieved herself of her burden, then turned to face her. "I need your help."

Olivia welcomed an opportunity to focus on something other than her own issues. "What's going on?"

Sam unclipped her walkie-talkie from her waistband. "I received a call from the Ecuadoran team. John Kingsley, their lead guide, appears to have come down with HACE. Members of his team are bringing him down now. The climb doctor at their BC wants to know if you'll confirm his diagnosis before he radios for an emergency medical evac."

Unlike HAPE, which affected the lungs, High Altitude Cerebral Edema affected the brain. Oxygen-deprived blood vessels began to leak, causing the brain to swell. As the intracranial pressure increased, the victim's mental and motor skills rapidly deteriorated.

"I'd be happy to help."

Olivia strode toward her tent to fetch her medical bag. She had to move fast. If he did have HACE, John wouldn't realize he was affected until it was too late. If he didn't descend immediately, he could lapse into a coma and die. She needed time to examine him, confirm or discount the initial doctor's diagnosis, and wait for the airlift to arrive if she felt an evacuation was warranted.

A few minutes later, four men carrying a fifth bundled inside a mummy-shaped sleeping bag appeared in camp. Sam introduced one of them as Graham West, John's longtime assistant. "Give me the details," Olivia said as she knelt next to John and began to examine him.

Graham ran a hand through his hair. "As long as I've known John—and Sam can back me up on this—he has never slept for more than four or five hours at a stretch. Yesterday, he slept for eighteen hours straight. At first, I didn't think anything of it. He was exhausted after we crossed the rock band. We all were. When he finally woke, he didn't seem himself. His speech was slurred and he stumbled around camp like he'd drunk two bottles of his favorite Scotch when I know for a fact he hasn't had a drop since we left BC. Now he's hallucinating and his vision's starting to fade."

"After blindness comes partial paralysis, seizures, unconsciousness, total paralysis, and coma." Olivia ticked the symptoms off on her fingers. "I don't need to tell you what comes after that."

She increased the output on John's canister of oxygen and gave him an injection of dexamethasone to temporarily alleviate his symptoms and prepare him for descent. His pulse was strong, but he was becoming increasingly lethargic.

"Radio your doctor at BC and tell him to get a chopper up here ASAP. We need to get this man off the mountain now."

"We're too high up," Sam said. "A chopper with a turbine engine can fly this high, but the air is too thin for it to hover. You'll need to descend much lower for a medical rescue."

"The boys and I will take him down to twelve thousand," Graham said. "Have the chopper meet us there."

"Roger that." Sam lifted the walkie-talkie to her mouth and made the call.

Olivia watched Graham and the other men begin their descent, a slow, treacherous race to meet the arriving helicopter. As the bird hovered above the ground, medical personnel would slowly lower a rescue basket. Graham or one of the other men would guide the litter to the ground, place John inside, and secure straps over his arms, legs, and chest. Then the rescue team would raise the basket and take John to Kathmandu so he could get the medical attention he needed.

Olivia couldn't stop imagining herself in John's place. In Chance's. In Marie-Eve's. In Bailey's.

Exhaustion set in as soon as Graham and the other men were out of sight. Olivia felt her legs begin to give way. As she sank to her knees in the snow, she finally lost her fragile hold on her emotions. Tears welled in her eyes. She tried to keep them from spilling over, but a dam had burst inside her and she was powerless to stem the tide.

How could she have been foolish enough to think she could conquer a mountain that had bested so many? Why had she even tried?

She was so tired. Tired of running. Tired of climbing. Tired of chasing impossible dreams.

She just wanted to stop.

Strong hands hauled her to her feet. An arm curled around her waist, holding her up.

Olivia blinked away her tears. When her eyes regained focus, Sam's wind-burned face filled her vision. The concern she saw radiating back at her was too much for her to handle.

"I can't do this," she said, breaking down again. "It's too much."

"No, it isn't. You're one of the strongest climbers I've ever seen. If you stop now, you'll regret it for the rest of your life. Keep going, Olivia. I know you can do it. And you won't have to do it alone. I'll be right by your side the whole time."

Olivia wrapped her arms around Sam's neck and, as she had been doing since the day they began the ascent, put her life in her hands.

CHAPTER ELEVEN

At base camp, Sam sat at the conference table and rubbed her hands over her face to try to pierce the fog shrouding her brain. Surprisingly, she was having more trouble concentrating at BC than on the mountain. Olivia's breakdown, though expected, had been difficult to see. Watching Olivia's emotions pour out of her had reaffirmed Sam's decision to keep hers under wraps, a decision that was proving easier to make than to keep. When Olivia had cried in her arms, she had wanted to hold her until she stopped. Instead, she had given her a pep talk and convinced her she had what it took to reach the summit. Convinced her of what her heart already knew but her mind had forced her to forget. Convinced her to keep going.

Unfortunately, Olivia wasn't the only one suffering from the physical and mental effects of their extended exertions. The entire group had taken quite a beating during the climb, herself included. They needed a break. Much longer than the three days of down time they would have before they began the summit push. But with more bad weather approaching, they didn't have time to waste.

"Sam?"

Sam started when Rae called her name. Was it the first time Rae had beckoned her or the twelfth?

"I'm sorry. What did you say?"

"When do you want to make the summit push?"

Sam reached across the table and spun the laptop in her direction. The forecast for the next ten days was displayed on the screen. The next five days were supposed to be clear. After that, however, the projections looked dicier. Another storm front was on the way. This one bigger than the last. According to the website, it was expected to blanket the mountain under at least three feet of snow and spawn wind gusts in excess of fifty miles an hour. Not Sam's idea of fun. Annapurna I was a formidable enough opponent on its own. It didn't need any help from the elements. If the storm was as bad as it appeared to be on the radar, help was definitely on the way.

"We packed up Camps One through Four on our way here, but we left Five and Six intact." She rubbed her chin as she thought out loud. "Today is Wednesday. If we ascend on Friday and bunk down at Camp Six for the night, we could try for the summit on Saturday. We won't have much time for photo ops, but we'll document our time at the top as best we can to make the attempt official. Then we'll descend to Camp Five that afternoon and do a rapid descent on Sunday. We have enough hands to pack up both remaining camps along the way. By the time the weather rolls in on Monday or Tuesday, we'll be safe and sound in Kathmandu."

"Your schedule's certainly ambitious," Rae said. "Do you think it's feasible?"

"After the initial blow, the storm's supposed to set in for a nice, long stay. If we don't go for the summit soon, we could be on hold for weeks, which would put the entire expedition in jeopardy. This team deserves to end on a high. They've had some tough times, but they've pulled together. They've bent a time or two, but they haven't broken. We're going to be cutting it close, but I think we can make it."

She took another look at the forecast and wondered if she was being too optimistic. Radar be damned, the weather on Annapurna I was notoriously unpredictable. The forecasters had been on target so far, but how much longer would their luck hold out?

Just five more days. That's all I need.

❖

In the dormitory-style bedroom, Olivia reclined on the cot she had earmarked as her own when they'd first arrived five weeks ago. She lay on her back, one arm covering her eyes. She was supposed to be resting, but her whirring brain wouldn't let her weary body shut down. The summit push was only a few days away. Her goal was within sight.

Her cell phone began to ring. Her hand, trained to respond to her chirping beeper no matter what the hour, reached for it reflexively. She brought the phone to her ear without bothering to check the display.

"Hello?"

"How's my second favorite physician in the whole wide world?"

"Chance." He sounded strong and vibrant. Nothing like the weakened man who hadn't been able to leave the mountain under his own power. She uncovered her face and gingerly sat up, one hand pressed against her tender ribs. "It is *so* good to hear your voice. How are you feeling?"

"A lot better than I was a few weeks ago, that's for sure. The team docs want me to sit out the first couple of games to make sure I'm back to full strength, but I feel like I'm already there. Gigi begs to differ."

"Gigi's right. I know you're anxious to get back on the court, but don't push yourself too hard. If you overdo it, you might have a relapse that could cost you the season rather than a handful of games."

"You and Gigi must practice your lines. That's the same thing she said."

"Great minds think alike. Unfortunately, they don't always follow their own advice."

"I hear you. Enough about me. I called to talk about you. How are you doing?"

She rubbed her side. "I've seen better days, but I'm hanging in there."

"You're almost home. In a few days, you'll be at the top."

"Weather permitting."

"How does it feel to be so close to your goal?"

"Anticlimactic."

"Why?"

"You and Gigi have been a part of this mission from the first day. I wish you were here to share the last one with me."

"So do I." The disappointment in his voice echoed her own. "I hope everything works out for you, Liv, but if it doesn't you'll always have me and Gigi in your corner. Hurry home, okay? We need to fire up the grill one more time before I put it in storage for the winter."

Olivia's mouth watered at the thought of a good old-fashioned backyard barbecue. "You pick up the steaks and I'll bring the beer."

"You got it."

Marie-Eve poked her head in the room to let her know it was her turn to see Dr. Curtis. He was performing physicals on each member of the team and Olivia was last in line.

"I've got to go, Chance. I'll talk to you soon, okay?"

"Sure thing. Be careful, okay?"

"Aren't I always? On second thought, don't answer that."

She ended the call and made her way to Dr. Nigel Curtis's makeshift office. She hopped on the examining table and tried not to flinch as he palpated her ribs.

She had grown accustomed to the dull ache in her side. She had managed to convince herself the pain was the byproduct of her body healing instead of breaking down, but she couldn't put a similar spin on the pronounced decrease in her energy level. The two good nights of sleep she'd gotten on the mountain and in base camp had helped replenish some of her physical reserves, but her emotional ones were still running on empty. Another two weeks of down time and she might be back to normal. Too bad she had only two more days.

"On a scale of one to ten, how would you rate your pain?" Nigel asked.

"Five on a good day. Eight on a bad one."

"And today?"

"Today's a six."

Nigel slipped his hands into the pockets of his rumpled gray cardigan. With his disheveled hair and wiry eyebrows, he looked like a cross between a kindly grandfather and a mad scientist. Mr. Rogers meets Albert Einstein. His soft-spoken demeanor put Olivia at ease. She hoped she had the same effect on her own patients. "You can get dressed now."

Olivia reached for her clothes. "Cracked or broken? What's the verdict?"

"Without an X-ray, I can't say for sure. One can logically assume, however, that if your rib was broken, the bone would be much more unstable than it is at present and you would be experiencing substantially more discomfort than you're reporting. I would say you have either a hairline fracture or a deep bruise. Unfortunately, there's no quick remedy for either. I could wrap your ribs to give them extra support while they mend, but the bindings would restrict your breathing. I would recommend that course of action if you were at sea level, not at altitude. When you resume the ascent, your oxygen levels will be low enough on their own without restricting your intake even more."

"What's your advice?" She thought she knew what he was going to say, but she asked the question nevertheless.

She looked at the medical equipment scattered around the room. Thermometers, blood pressure cuffs, heating pads, and rolls of gauze littered the landscape. Various medicines from aspirin to morphine were housed in a lightweight but sturdy safe. Nigel locked the safe and pocketed the key.

"Keep managing the pain and don't do anything foolish."

Olivia's short bark of laughter sent a jolt of pain through her ribs. She held on to the edge of the examining table to keep from keeling over. "Foolish as in climbing a mountain?"

Nigel arched one untamed eyebrow. "Or falling off one." His lined face creased into a concerned frown. "Please remember what I said."

"I'll be careful. I promise."

She ran into Sam outside Nigel's makeshift examining room.

Sam looked at her warily as she rubbed her side. "Are you injured?"

Olivia forced herself to drop her hand. She didn't want to appear weak in front of someone so strong. Then again, Sam had shown signs of weakness during the climb, too. She had been understandably emotional the day Jimmy had found Sanath—and the night she had told Olivia about Bailey. She had seemed like a machine when she was climbing, but she had proved all too human when she wasn't.

Now, though, her demeanor seemed dispassionate. Almost clinical. She had been distant since their return to BC. Since her fall on the ice ridge.

"My ribs hurt like hell," Olivia said, "but they haven't gotten any worse since we were swept up in the avalanche two weeks ago. What I'm experiencing now is nothing more than the normal wear and tear of an adventure like this. Were you looking for me?"

"No, but there is something I want to talk to you about. Take a walk with me."

Sam led her out of the tent and away from camp. They neared the outdoor shower. Olivia knew from memory the portable unit was cozy yet roomy. Its interior was four feet wide and just over seven feet tall, its polyurethane-coated walls providing privacy for its inhabitant. Two small skylights were placed in the domed roof for illumination. The overhead reservoir was filled with enough water for a brief but thoroughly satisfying shower. Yesterday, Olivia had refilled the five-gallon tank not once but twice. Today, if she had her way, she might break that record.

Rae poked her head out of the portable unit's D-shaped door and took a tentative step outside, a large towel loosely wrapped around her body.

"Where do you think you're going?" Marie-Eve reached for the towel. "Get back in here."

Rae squealed when her covering began to slip. She scurried inside and zipped the door shut. Even from thirty feet away, Olivia heard their laughter gradually evolve into moans.

"Sounds like someone's having fun," Sam said under her breath.

"What did you want to talk about?" Olivia asked after they were out of range.

"You."

Olivia had figured as much. "What about me?"

"How are you doing?"

"Like I said, I have a few aches and pains, but I'm fine."

"I don't mean physically. You had a frightening experience on the ice ridge and an emotional reaction to it after the fact. I need to know if you're okay to continue."

Olivia remembered the breakdown she had suffered the day before their return to BC. She remembered the pain and confusion she had felt. And she remembered Sam stepping in to alleviate both.

She had felt carefree in Sam's arms. As if the troubles she had faced during the expedition didn't matter. As if nothing else mattered except being held by Sam.

She would love to re-create the moments she had spent in Sam's arms, but the warmth she had felt during that brief period had long since turned cold.

It was as if they were still complete strangers instead of two people who had been working hand-in-hand every day for over a month. Two people who had experienced life and death and almost everything in between.

For weeks, they had grown inexorably closer. Now Sam seemed miles away. Olivia longed to close the gap, but not if it cost her a chance to reach the summit. She and Sam could resume telling each other their life stories later. Until then, she had a mountain to climb.

"We'll be retracing our steps on our way to the summit," Sam said. "Are you feeling any trepidation about climbing the ridge again?"

"No. As a matter of fact, I'm looking forward to the challenge." She needed to regain the sense of control she had lost when the broken rope had sent her skidding down the ice. She needed to reach the top. "You don't need to worry about me, Sam. The only thing you need to worry about is the weather. I hear there's another storm rolling in. Do you think it might disrupt our plans?"

Sam visibly relaxed at the change in subject. "I'm not going to sugarcoat it. A sizeable storm is a few days out. We can still make the summit on this climb, but our window of opportunity is a small one. We'll have to hustle or the window will slam shut before we know it. We'll be stuck waiting out the storm if the conditions get too rough, or if the mountain is deemed unsafe, we'll be forced to abandon the attempt entirely."

Olivia's heart sank. Before they descended to base, they had come within twenty-five hundred feet of the summit. Was that as close as they would get?

"Can you get us to the top?" she asked.

"Yes."

Sam's eyes glowed with steely determination. Olivia couldn't help but be inspired.

"I believe you."

"You won't regret it."

"No," Olivia said. "I don't think I will."

CHAPTER TWELVE

On Thursday, Sam gathered the slides and photographs she needed for her presentation then clapped her hands to get everyone's attention.

"Congratulations," she said after the conference room gradually fell quiet. "You're only a few hours away from reaching the summit." She paused as everyone applauded, stomped, and cheered. The climbers' excitement was so infectious she felt her own adrenaline surge. "We'll begin our ascent tomorrow at four a.m. If we keep a steady pace, we should make it to Camp Six by early afternoon. We'll have something to eat, then rest up for Saturday. Saturday is summit day."

The resulting roar was so loud her ears rang. The remaining members of Olivia's team exchanged high fives. Marie-Eve, as exuberant as always, led the celebration. Peter held up the tiny camera he used to record his vlogs. He slowly panned the room, capturing the moving images of everyone in it. If Sam had known he'd planned on filming the meeting, she would have combed her hair with something other than her fingers.

"Get plenty of sleep tomorrow night. On Saturday, we're going to be moving fast in order to stay ahead of this."

She flipped on the overhead projector. A colorful slide of the enormous weather cell slowly making its way over the Himalayas appeared on the wall. Olivia gasped at the size of the storm. Sam sneaked a glance at her. The storm was obviously preoccupying her thoughts at the moment, but Sam wondered what else was on her mind. Was she more concerned by the prospect of encountering the approaching squall or making another attempt to climb the ice ridge?

Out here, fear could be your best friend or your worst enemy. It kept you alert, preventing silly mistakes, but it could also retard performance. Sam hoped Olivia wouldn't freeze up when she returned to the site where she had nearly lost her life.

"Tonight, I want you to go through your backpacks and remove everything except the most essential items. Take nothing except what you'll need to get you to the summit. On these final legs, the snow will be deep and the terrain taxing. You'll want to be carrying as little weight as possible. Leave the extraneous items behind. Rae and Roland will keep them safe while you're gone. You can reclaim them when we return from the summit."

Marie-Eve raised her hand. "What items do you suggest we take?"

"Rae and I will provide the food and equipment—helmets, goggles, sleeping bags, lanterns, ropes, oxygen, carabiners, first aid kits. Aside from lightweight warm clothing, you'll need to bring only toiletries."

"Good deal."

"Before I forget, the flight to Kathmandu is scheduled to leave at four p.m. on Sunday. The chopper is large enough to seat our entire party, so there's no need to argue over preferred departure times. As for deciding who gets a window seat, I'm afraid you're on your own. Rock-paper-scissors always works for me. Does anyone else have any questions?"

Peter raised his hand. "Assuming it will take us four to five hours to descend from the summit, that means we'll need to begin the return trip no later than eleven a.m. That doesn't leave us much time to spend at the summit. How long do you think we'll remain at the apex?"

"That depends on three factors—the time we arrive, the weather conditions when we get there, and the distance between our fastest and slowest climbers." She tried to move on before he could ask her to be more specific. "Anyone else?"

"What's your best guess?"

Peter's follow-up question made her feel like a politician at a press conference. She wanted to stick to the prepared script while he sought to steer her down the path he wanted her to take. She wanted to talk about the journey, not the destination. The time spent at the summit was the briefest part of the ascent. Climbers wanted to set up camp and stay all day, savoring their accomplishment for as long as they could. Guides felt the pressure to keep them moving. To make room for the next group waiting to take their places. To get them down the mountain and safely back to BC as soon as possible. She didn't want to dampen the team's spirits by telling them all the long hours they had spent training and planning wouldn't have an extended payoff, but Peter was forcing her to do just that.

"We'll have an hour at the summit, two at the most."

Peter and Marie-Eve grumbled in protest. Exactly what Sam feared would happen if Peter pursued this line of questioning. She raised her hands to silence the murmurs.

"I'll give you three choices," she said when she was sure she had regained everyone's attention. "Each of you can spend an hour at the summit and have the rest of your lives to talk about the experience, you can miss out on making it to the top altogether, or you can freeze to death in a blizzard and spend the rest of eternity up there."

The protests quickly came to an end.

"It's my job to make hard decisions. Though they're not always popular ones, they're usually the right ones."

"I think I speak for all of us," Olivia said evenly, "when I say an hour at the summit is plenty of time."

Olivia's soothing voice calmed the growing tension. When Olivia's eyes met hers, Sam nodded her thanks for the save. Olivia's chin lifted ever so slightly in acknowledgment.

"Each of you will be given two canisters of oxygen on summit day," Sam continued. "Enough for twelve hours of air. Running out of oxygen and descending to Camp Six unaided is not a recommended course of action. Therefore, I suggest we remain at the summit only as long as necessary to complete the tasks needed to make the climb official. You're going to be fighting both the mountain and the elements. I don't want you to be at war with your own bodies as well." She took a breath. "As I said at the beginning of this trip, most accidents happen on the descent, not the climb. After you reach the summit, you're going to be exhausted, exhilarated, then deflated. When the realization hits that the primary goal of this mission has been achieved and there's nothing left to accomplish other than going home, I'd rather you experience that moment closer to BC."

"I have a question," Olivia said. "Has your team installed fixed ropes all the way to the summit or will we be forced to wait while the task is completed? As I'm sure you're well aware, fixed ropes are a necessity on vertical faces and steep inclines. The installation, however, could cause a delay we can't afford under the circumstances."

"Agreed," Sam said. When Olivia's eyes drifted toward the projection of the oncoming storm, she followed her gaze. She turned off the projector. Trying to seem casual and relaxed, she tried to restore Olivia's confidence. "Jimmy supervised the installation of fixed ropes during a successful summit of Annapurna I earlier this year. Those ropes should still be intact. If they aren't, it shouldn't take long to make the necessary repairs. In case repairs are necessary, each member of the support team will carry one hundred feet of fresh rope in their backpacks. I don't anticipate the additional coils will end up being used, but better to have them and not need them than need them and not have them."

Olivia's face blanched. Sam wondered if she was remembering the fixed ropes breaking on the ice ridge. Sam thanked her lucky stars every night that Olivia's accident hadn't resulted in serious injury. During the fall, Olivia could have easily broken an arm, a leg, or even her neck. Instead, the only fracture was to their burgeoning relationship. A tradeoff Sam was more than willing to accept.

"Get lots of shut eye tonight. I'll see you in the morning."

Olivia followed her team members out of the tent after the meeting adjourned. She knew they should probably heed Sam's admonition to get plenty of rest before tomorrow's ascent, but she was too keyed up to sleep. She followed Peter, Pasang, and Marie-Eve to the series of sal stumps that circled a small fire.

"What are you most looking forward to about going home?" Pasang asked.

"Being able to breathe without an oxygen tank strapped to my back," Peter said.

"Being warm," Marie-Eve said as she took a seat next to Olivia. "I've been freezing ever since Jimmy and Lhakpa dug me up after the avalanche. What about you, Doc?"

"Crowds." Olivia warmed her hands by the fire. "At one time, I thought I could never feel lonelier than in a roomful of strangers. Now I know better. Out here, I feel like we're the last people on earth."

"I know what you mean." Marie-Eve turned uncharacteristically introspective. "Before yesterday, I was yearning for a connection. Fortunately, I was able to find one."

"Yeah, I heard. You and Rae put on quite a show."

Marie-Eve hid her crimson cheeks inside the turned-up collar of her thick down parka.

Olivia turned to watch Sam supervise the loading of the surplus furniture and equipment into a compact tractor-trailer. As each item passed by, she ticked them off on an inventory sheet. Pretty soon, the only things left would be the tent over their heads and the cots underneath their butts.

As the last of the folding chairs disappeared into the back of the truck, Sam turned as if she could sense being observed. Her eyes bore into Olivia's. Olivia resisted the urge to turn away. She tried to decipher the quizzical look on Sam's face.

How did Sam see her? As a favored client, a delicate flower that needed protecting, or a woman who piqued her interest? At times, she felt like all three, but she didn't know which role suited her best. Perhaps one day she'd have time to find out.

As she continued to meet Sam's gaze, she felt something stir in her—a flicker of desire that quickly burst into flame. Perhaps the time was now.

Chapter Thirteen

S am was so worn out she barely tasted dinner, a joint effort from Pasang and Roland that, based on the rate at which it disappeared, must have been delicious. She fell into bed exhausted but couldn't fall asleep. In her head, she kept visualizing the route for tomorrow's ascent—and replaying the look Olivia gave her while she was loading the truck. The look had been an odd mixture of idle curiosity and naked desire. Was Olivia on the hunt for a random hook-up similar to Rae and Marie-Eve's or was she looking for something that would last longer than it took for the water in the outdoor shower to run dry?

Sam didn't know if she could provide either. She had dabbled in her fair share of one-night stands over the years—evenings that often began with a look and always ended with a promise not often kept to keep in touch—but this felt different.

If she allowed herself to give in to the desire she felt for Olivia, she didn't think she'd be able to say good-bye when the long, dark night turned into day.

Sam bunched up her pillow, rolled over on her side, and tried to convince herself the point was moot.

Just three more days, she told herself as she tried to force sleep to come. *In three more days, you'll never have to see Olivia Bradshaw again.*

The thought didn't provide the comfort she longed for. Far from it.

Giving up on sleep, she pulled on her boots, grabbed her jacket, and headed outside, the powerful beam of her headlamp guiding the way.

She took a seat on the sal stump where she had ridden out many a restless night. She took a deep breath of the crisp mountain air and tried to will away her anxiety. It had been years since she had felt this out of sorts before a summit push. Her team was ready. Of that, she had no doubt. Jimmy and Lhakpa were exceptional climbers, and Pasang had proven himself to be equally adept. His performance during the first part of the expedition had earned him a well-deserved shot at the summit.

No, it wasn't her team but Olivia's that concerned her. Specifically, Olivia herself.

Marie-Eve and Peter seemed ready for the challenges the next few days would bring. Olivia said she was, too, but Sam wouldn't truly believe her until they made it past the ice ridge. Maybe then she could finally relax.

Stop fooling yourself.

She blew out a sigh. She wouldn't be able to relax until Olivia Bradshaw was either in her arms or thousands of miles away—well out of arm's reach.

Sam stared up at the night sky, but instead of the stars, her attraction to Olivia was the focus of her examinations.

Olivia was obviously beautiful, but her physical attributes weren't the only reason Sam was drawn to her. She cared about other people's well-being so much she was willing to put her own at risk in order to raise money for their medical care. Not only that. Watching her put her medical expertise to work was exciting and incredibly sexy.

Sam liked women who were confident and in control. When Olivia treated a patient—Chance after he collapsed from HAPE, Marie-Eve after she was buried in the snow, John after he came down with HACE, even Peter's nosebleed and Pasang's head laceration—she had seemed all-powerful.

But her compassion was always in evidence. She appeared to have genuine concern for the people in her care. To her, they were people not cases.

Sam sighed again. If Olivia's healing hands touched her, would they be able to remove the thick layers of scar tissue that had formed over her heart? Despite her obvious skill, Sam doubted even Olivia could pull off an operation that complex.

"Why am I not surprised to find you here?"

Sam's wounded heart raced at the sound of Olivia's voice, raspy and low from the lateness of the hour. If this was how she sounded first thing in the morning, Sam wanted to wake up with her every day.

"Can't sleep?" she asked as Olivia took a seat next to her.

"I can't wait to get going."

Sam glanced at her watch. The slowly revolving hands glowed in the dark. "We've got another two and a half hours before we shove off."

"I know. I've been staring at the clock for the past forty-five minutes. I figured the view was better out here. I also thought I'd be first in line for the shower, but I don't mind sharing if you want to conserve water."

Olivia's broad grin let Sam know she was kidding, but that didn't keep the pleasant thought of showering with Olivia from entering her mind. Slowly soaping Olivia's body, kneading the fatigue from her muscles, stoking her desire while she cried out for more.

"We've had a slew of problems during this expedition," Olivia said.

The sudden shift in subjects helped Sam regain the focus she had lost the second she had heard Olivia's voice calling to her in the dark. Beckoning to her like a siren to a sailor. "I've seen worse," she said, trying to avoid being dashed on the rocks rushing toward her.

"What kind of grade would you give this trip, a C or a D?"

"Any trip in which the majority of the group reaches the summit and no one gets hurt deserves an A in my book."

"How many trips have you made?"

"Up Annapurna or in general?"

"Either."

Sam shrugged. "More than I can count."

"Ball park."

"I do an average of four climbs a year. Over a course of ten years, that adds up to forty climbs, give or take."

"Impressive. How long do you think you'll keep at it?"

"If my body holds out, I plan to keep this up for at least another ten years or so."

"And then?"

Olivia leaned forward as if hearing the answer to her question was the most important thing in the world. The look she had given Sam earlier had returned. This time, her curiosity was mixed with a different kind of desire. A desire for knowledge. If Sam wasn't careful, this woman would unearth all her secrets. The strange thing was she didn't want to be careful. She had already told Olivia about Mont Blanc—the secret she had tried to bury in the past. Now that the past had come to light, what was left to hold her back? Only herself. Her lingering guilt over the role she had played in Bailey's accident kept her from moving on with her life. She needed to get out of her own way, but she didn't know how. She had forgiven Bailey for making the choices she had made, but she couldn't forgive herself for the decisions she had made.

Part of her wanted to share her dreams with Olivia; part of her wanted to keep them to herself. What began as idle conversation had turned personal. Did she dare open a door best left closed? Fighting her own uncertainty, she turned the knob.

"I had some good times in Mexico. I've always thought I'd go back one day and open a bar on the beach. The kind of place locals frequent but isn't listed on most visitors' guides. My own version of Cheers but with umbrella drinks instead of Sam Adams."

"Sounds like a place I'd love to hang out in. I'll have to look you up so I can ride a bar stool all day wearing a sarong and a bikini."

"What about you?" Sam asked, feeling a bit curious herself. "Can you see yourself as anything other than a doctor?"

"When I was a kid, I wanted to be a basketball player when I grew up, but my jump shot is nowhere near as reliable as Chance's. Now I can't imagine myself as anything other than what I am. I plan to keep practicing until I keel over or someone kicks me out of the OR, whichever comes first. Now back to you. Besides climbing Shishapangma, what's on your bucket list?"

"The usual things. To see the sun set from the top of the Empire State Building. To watch the sun rise over a glacier in Antarctica. To go to Rio during Carnival. To visit New Orleans during Mardi Gras. To have a picnic under the Northern Lights."

"And? Your list seems incomplete."

"I want to give more than I take. Relax more and worry less. The usual things. What about you?"

"All things considered, I've led a rather charmed life. I've had more ups than downs and more good days than bad. I've accomplished more than I ever thought I would and gotten myself into and out of scrapes I initially considered impossible to escape. But by far the most magical moment I've ever had is—"

"Climbing Annapurna?"

"Sitting here with you. Enjoying the simple pleasures of life—talking about whatever comes to mind, experiencing the joy of discovery. I had forgotten how much fun those things could be. Thank you for reminding me."

"You're welcome."

Olivia sat back, a satisfied look on her face. "I think this is the longest conversation we've had since we met."

"It's definitely the longest I've seen you sit still. Why are you always in such a hurry? Afraid you're going to miss something?"

Olivia's smile faltered a bit as if Sam had stumbled upon a sensitive subject. "I want to experience as many things as I can. The faster I can get from Point A to Point B, the faster I can move on to something else."

Sam wondered if Olivia treated the women in her life just as matter-of-factly. Another reason to stay far, far away.

"The faster you move on, the less time you have to savor what you've just accomplished. The experience you'll have on Sunday is one you don't want to rush. Do yourself a favor. Savor every moment."

"And then?"

"That's up to you." Sam pushed herself to her feet. "I'm going to try to catch twenty winks before breakfast. What about you?"

"I'm right behind you."

Olivia followed Sam inside. She didn't think she could sleep if she tried, but she finally drifted off around three a.m. Just in time for Marie-Eve's ringing alarm clock to jolt her awake again. She blinked in the pre-dawn dark, waiting for her eyes to adjust to the lack of light.

"Up and at 'em, sunshine," Marie-Eve said cheerily. "It's go time."

Olivia heard rustles, groans, and gentle whispers as the others began to stir. She tossed off her covers, swung her legs over the side of her cot, and stepped into her boots. She yawned long and loud as she vigorously rubbed her face with her hands.

"Where's your get up and go?" Marie-Eve asked.

"It got up and went." Olivia stood and stretched. Her joints popped like a string of lit firecrackers.

"I hope that felt better than it sounded."

She squeezed a line of toothpaste onto the bristles of her brush. Then she grabbed a bottle of mineral water and wandered outside as she brushed her teeth.

The campsite teemed with activity. While Marie-Eve and Peter ate protein-rich energy bars to fortify themselves for the upcoming journey, Jimmy and the rest of the Sherpas checked the climbing equipment and supplies. Sam supervised their efforts.

Olivia spat out the toothpaste and took a swig of water. She rinsed her mouth before draining the bottle. She tossed the plastic container in a recycling bin and wiped her mouth with the back of her hand. She still felt half-asleep. The conversation she'd shared with Sam felt like the remnants of a dream. Sam had opened up to her for the first time in weeks. The more Olivia learned about her, the more she wanted to know.

The solitary nature of Sam's current profession seemed at odds with her plans for the future, but both seemed to suit her personality. Olivia could easily imagine her climbing mountains for another decade, then giving it up to sling drinks and share her stories. Olivia wanted to hear them all. Hopefully, she wouldn't have to wait ten years to get started.

Talking with Sam had felt like one of those moments Sam had told her about. The kind she was supposed to savor. Olivia had wanted to sit with her all night. Talk with her until the sun rose. For once, she had wanted to stop searching for the next experience and simply enjoy the one at hand. Sometimes she wondered if her constant search for the next goal, the next thrill would ever end. How much was enough? Would anything—anyone—ever be enough to make her put down roots instead of constantly testing her wings? Last night, Sam had made her feel like the answer was yes.

Olivia went back inside, grabbed her oversized backpack, and headed to what was left of the conference room. The space had been practically gutted. The only items that remained were several pieces of radio equipment, a laptop, and two director's chairs. Olivia eyed the comfortable perches from which Rae and her new sidekick Roland would monitor the climb. Comfort aside, she'd rather be on the mountain than relegated to BC.

She taped one of her business cards to the front of her backpack so Rae and Roland would be able to differentiate it from the other bags lining the canvas walls. She searched the small rucksack she used for short hikes. Short, in this case, being treks that lasted a few hours instead of a few weeks. The bag also doubled as a carry-on during plane flights. Instead of a change of clothes and an extra pair of underwear, this time the bag was packed with toiletries, sunscreen, sunglasses, and a digital camera, in addition to her passport, medical bag, and cell phone.

Sitting cross-legged on the floor, she unzipped the rucksack's middle compartment and pulled out her diary. She had taken time to make entries during each leg, recording her experiences while they were fresh on her mind so they wouldn't get lost in the haze of memory.

She opened the book to the page she had marked after her last entry. Holding her pen cap between her teeth, she tried to describe the various emotions churning through her body.

Friday, November 8
3:50 A.M.

Today is the day I've been looking forward to for well over a year. In a few precious moments, Sam and her team will lead us back up the mountain. By this time tomorrow, we'll be preparing to climb the summit. I'm recording my thoughts now because I don't know how clear my head will be in twenty-four hours. Supplemental oxygen is an aid, not a cure-all. After we reach Camp Six, I'm sure my brain will be as foggy as a late afternoon in San Francisco.

Time prohibits me from listing all their names now, but each person who has played a part in the planning, organization, and execution of this climb has had a hand in its success thus far. Here's hoping nothing happens in the next few days to change the expected rosy outcome.

When I arrive in Kathmandu, the two questions I expect to be asked the most are Was it worth it? and Would you do it again? At the moment, I don't know the answer to either query.

I expected the trip to be challenging. So far, it has exceeded my expectations. I have never felt as frightened as I do right now. I want to reach the summit more than I've wanted anything in my life except my degree, but I can't do it unless I cross the ice ridge. I experienced equipment failure on my first attempt at traversing that treacherous patch of ice. In my head, I know the chances of something similar occurring today are remote. My heart, however, isn't so easily convinced.

I've always prided myself on my endurance and mental toughness. Both have been sorely tested during my time in Nepal. Both will be tested even more over the next few days. I hope I'm ready for the challenge. If I am, I will prove that I can withstand more, do more, be more than I ever thought I could. And if I'm not, I suspect the disappointment will be crushing—both for me and for those rooting for me to succeed. People are counting on me to make it to the top. I have to do my best not to screw it up.

Sam Murphy is the woman who can get me there. Our time together will come to an end in a few days, but I'm not ready to say good-bye to her yet. I enjoy the talks we have about subjects both serious and silly. I even enjoy her quiet periods that used to drive me crazy at the beginning of this trip.

She has issues to work through. Don't we all? Part of me wants to let her face her demons in her own way in her own time, but part of me wants to help her fight through the pain. All of me wants to see what she's like when she comes out the other side.

"There you are."

Olivia was so focused on completing her journal entry she hadn't heard Rae and Roland enter the room.

"Everyone's waiting for you," Rae said.

"You haven't changed your mind, have you?" Roland asked.

"No, of course not." She looked at her watch. Ten minutes after four. Her burst of inspiration had thrown everyone off schedule. "I got busy and lost track of time. Sorry." She stuffed her journal into her bag and scrambled to her feet.

"I'll call off the search party." Rae lifted her walkie-talkie to her mouth. "I've got her, Sam. She's in the conference room."

"Send her my way so we can get this show on the road."

Sam's reply was terse, her voice gruff. Exactly the response Olivia had expected. Rae's indulgent smile, however, seemed to indicate she shouldn't take Sam's brusque manner to heart.

Could Sam and Rae be any more different? Rae was quick to laugh. Her easy-going manner put Olivia at ease. Sam, on the other hand, was so tightly wound she kept Olivia on edge. But it was Sam's face not Rae's that she saw when she closed her eyes at night. It was Sam not Rae who fueled her fantasies, appeared in her dreams. Would her dreams ever become reality?

She mouthed more apologies as Rae waved her out of the room.

"Good luck," Roland said. He slipped a pair of bulky radio operator headphones over his ears. "We'll be listening."

"She should be at your twenty in a tick," Olivia heard Rae say into her walkie-talkie.

"Roger that."

As she jogged toward the rendezvous point, Olivia felt like a truant who had been rounded up and summoned to the principal's office. She feared her punishment might be much worse than a few days in detention.

Sam wasn't much of a talker to begin with. Whenever she was upset with someone, Olivia had noticed, she didn't yell or scream. She stopped talking to them altogether. Olivia loved open lines of communication. For her, no sanction was worse than the silent treatment. Being ignored by the person whose attention you sought the most was a fate worse than any other.

"Glad you could join us," Sam said after Olivia skidded to a stop.

Sam's expression was neutral. Olivia couldn't tell if she was being jovial or mocking. Despite the many hours they'd spent together, Sam was becoming harder to read instead of easier. She pinballed from approachable to standoffish to tortured. When she began to lead everyone up the mountain, she assumed her most common persona—no-nonsense and all business. Once they cleared the crevasse near Camp One, she sent Jimmy and Pasang ahead to scout the next part of the route. Then she set a strong pace for everyone else to follow.

Lhakpa positioned himself at the rear of the pack, Olivia in the middle. Peter and Marie-Eve were about ten yards in front of her. As conditioning became a factor, Olivia passed the slower climbers with ease. By the time they made it to what had once been Camp Three, she was right on Sam's shoulder.

"What took you so long?" Sam asked. "I was expecting you hours ago."

Sam was so hard to read Olivia couldn't tell if her comment was a jibe or a rare attempt at humor. She chose to treat it as the latter instead of the former. "I was savoring the moment, I guess."

Sam walked pitched slightly forward to compensate for the weight of her backpack and the steepness of the slope. She looked—and sounded—like she had a dilapidated VW Beetle on her back. The pack's wide straps dug into her shoulders. Metal clanked against metal each time she moved.

"Would you like me to carry your bag for a while?" Olivia asked.

"Thanks, but I can manage."

Olivia was surprised to see a smile tug at the corner of Sam's mouth, a refreshing change from the serious countenance she had sported all morning. She smiled, too. "What's so funny?"

"You." Sam shifted her backpack, providing a metallic score to her words. "You sound like you're offering to carry my books while you walk me home from school."

The comment conjured images of a more innocent time. Of shared milkshakes at the corner ice cream parlor and jagged initials carved into the bark of a tree. The images warmed Olivia's heart.

When she looked up at the ice ridge, however, she felt a chill that had nothing to do with the frigid temperatures.

On paper, the challenges that lay ahead were more difficult than the one they currently faced, but the ice wall and rock bands didn't strike nearly as much fear in her as the ice ridge.

When they reached the base of the ridge, Sam set her backpack on the ground and flexed her shoulders. Olivia could almost hear the stressed ligaments sighing in relief.

"Are we working in the same teams as last time?" she asked, noticing Jimmy was positioned above the ridge while Pasang remained at its base.

"Yes." Sam briefly squeezed her shoulder. "I meant what I said, Olivia. You don't have to do this alone. I'll be with you the whole way. Lhakpa and Marie-Eve will go up together. Peter and Pasang will follow. Then you and I will join them."

Olivia nodded. Sam's assurance and quiet confidence gave her the courage to face her fears. No way would she let this mountain beat her.

Sam reached for her walkie-talkie. "Jimmy, check in," she said in Nepali. "How does it look up there?"

"We're clear all the way to the ice wall. I'm headed to the rock band now."

"Are you ready for me to send the first team your way?"

"Ready."

"Roger that. Get everyone moving again as soon as they catch their breath after scaling the ridge. We're making good time and I want to take advantage of it. The sooner we get to Camp Six, the better." Sam switched to English. Olivia admired her ability to make seamless shifts between languages and cultures. "Lhakpa. Marie-Eve. You're up. Let's go."

Sam pulled on each of the fixed ropes to test their strength. They looked solid enough. Then again, they had the last time, too, before one had snapped and sent Olivia plummeting down the embankment.

Lhakpa and Marie-Eve quickly climbed the ridge. Pasang and Peter followed. After both pairs reached the top, Sam hooked her arms through her backpack's shoulder straps and cinched a third strap around her waist. When empty, the pack weighed about ten pounds. Fully loaded as it was now, it weighed closer to fifty.

Olivia backed away, her courage abandoning her.

"You're one of the strongest people I've ever met in my life," Sam said. She guided Olivia forward, clipped her ascender to one of the reinforced nylon ropes, and gave Olivia's helmet a gentle tap. "Now get up there and prove to yourself what I already know."

Sam began to push herself up the ridge one step at a time. Despite the added burden of her overloaded backpack, she climbed at a comfortable pace. Not too fast, but not too slow. Olivia followed her lead, her heart in her throat the entire time. True to her word, Sam was right next to her every step of the way.

When they neared the top, Olivia felt a combination of excitement, trepidation, and fear. This was the point where everything had gone wrong during the first half of the ascent. Would it happen again?

Sam seemed to sense her doubts.

"Keep pushing," she said quietly. "We're almost there."

Gripping the rope with all her might, Olivia dug her crampon into the ice to improve her footing. Then she continued to climb hand-over-hand, step-by-step until the top of the ridge was within reach. Instead of waiting for Sam to unhook and offer her a hand up, Olivia hauled herself over the edge of the ridge.

When she stood on level ground for the first time in hours, her heart hammered in her chest. From exertion, excitement, and exhilaration. She had done it. She had conquered the demon that had bedeviled her for days. She hoped reaching the summit would feel as good as it did to be standing above the crest that would haunt her dreams no more.

"Good job," Sam said with her usual verbal economy.

"Come on," Olivia said, feeling like her old self again. "I'll race you to the top."

CHAPTER FOURTEEN

Olivia went to bed early but didn't get much sleep. In less than eight hours, they would try for the summit. In a little more than twelve hours, she would fulfill a longtime dream. If the weather held.

The wind was growing progressively worse by the minute. Intermittent gusts howled through camp as the weather system they hoped to avoid crept inexorably closer. If they didn't make it to the top tomorrow, they would have to abandon the attempt.

Olivia pulled her sleeping bag up to her chin. Even though her earplugs muffled most of the sound, she could still hear the walls of the tent flapping in the wind. She hoped the tent stakes had been driven deep enough to hold. If the pegs were set too shallowly, she, Marie-Eve, and Sam could be blown off the mountain.

She turned on her headlamp long enough to check the gauge on her oxygen canister. This one was half full. Enough for three more hours of air. She turned off the light and tried to slow her racing mind.

Sam stirred in her sleep and moaned softly. Was she dreaming of Bailey and that day on Mont Blanc? Logic would seem to say so.

Olivia longed to stroke Sam's hair and take away her pain, but there were some wounds even she couldn't heal.

❖

Sam jerked awake. She'd had the dream again. The one that forced her to relive the few seconds that had preyed on her mind for years. Tonight, the dream seemed worse somehow. The images were the same, but the feelings they stirred up struck her with more force than usual.

She held her head in her hands. Memories of Bailey would continue to haunt her as long as she allowed them to. She had to take control of her life before she lost her grip on the reins.

She crawled outside and headed for the communications tent. The luminescent dial on her watch read two forty-five a.m. When she located the radio, she keyed the microphone three times before raising it to her mouth.

"Summit camp to BC. Come in, BC."

"Someone's off to a quick start this morning," Rae said when her voice finally came on the radio. "Do you have a hot date waiting for you in Kat or something?"

"No, I want to make sure we're okay to go before everyone begins to stir." Sam lowered the volume to keep from disturbing the sleeping campers. "I don't want them to get their hopes up for nothing. There's no need to get them ready now if we're going to be stuck here for a few more hours. How does the weather look?"

"Give me a sec. I'm pulling up the forecast now. The hour-by-hour still looks good for today and tomorrow."

Sam breathed a sigh of relief. Though they were still on schedule, they weren't entirely out of danger. "If this wind keeps up, one of us is going to have a bumpy flight to Kathmandu."

"I'll flip you for it. Winner rides in the chopper, loser rides shotgun with Jimmy in the truck. Heads or tails?"

Without knowing whether Rae planned to flip a quarter, a rand, a rupee, or a Euro, Sam didn't know which side of the coin in Rae's hand was heavier and, therefore, more likely to land on top. She went with her gut. "Heads."

Sam heard a slapping sound as Rae caught the coin and pressed it against her forearm. "Tails. You lose. Enjoy your ride."

"I will. Enjoy your flight."

"The way Jimmy drives, you'll probably make it to Kat before we do. Give me a shout when you get to the summit."

"Will do. Over and out."

Jimmy stuck his head out of his tent and looked at her inquisitively. She gave him a thumbs-up sign, indicating they were a go. He ducked back inside. He reappeared a few minutes later with Lhakpa and Pasang in tow. After the three wolfed down a breakfast of Tibetan tea and two bowls of gruel, Jimmy and Lhakpa left to scout the route. The climbers began to spill out of their tents shortly afterward.

"Ready or not," Sam said under her breath. "Here we go."

An hour after they cleared the last crevasse, they entered the death zone, the point above twenty-six thousand feet at which there wasn't sufficient oxygen to sustain human life for longer than a few hours. Without supplemental oxygen, high altitude sickness would quickly set in. Medical rescues at the summit were too risky due to the strong, unpredictable winds. A stricken climber would have to find the strength to descend on his own or, like John Kingsley, be carried by able-bodied friends.

Olivia checked the gauge on her first oxygen canister. She had enough remaining air to make it to the summit and out of the death zone before she would have to switch. Good. The conditions were too rough to make the change now.

She clung to the fixed rope as the wind buffeted her body. Her boots, laden with melted snow and ice, felt like they were made of lead. Reminding herself that her long quest was almost over helped ease the burden. Adrenaline kicked in, flooding her body with much-needed energy. She felt like sprinting to the top, but she somehow managed to convince herself to take her time.

She was at the head of the pack. Only Sam would make it to the summit before she would. Jimmy and Lhakpa were already there.

Four hundred feet. Three hundred. Two.

She passed makeshift memorials erected to honor the lives of the fallen. She paused to acknowledge their loss. Her group had been fortunate. They had suffered through unexpected departures and endured more than one close call, but all had survived the attempt. So far. If Sam was right—if leaving the summit was more treacherous than reaching it—the worst was yet to come.

One hundred feet. Fifty.

Olivia could see the peak and the sky beyond it. With one last push, she was standing on the summit. She was standing on the top of the most dangerous mountain in the world. She thrust her arms in the air as Jimmy and Lhakpa applauded her achievement. Sam was there, too, but she didn't join the celebration. She stood stone-faced, her eyes focused on the other climbers still making their way up the mountain.

Olivia tried to make the most of her brief time at the top. She stood with her legs spread far apart, bracing herself against the wind. She looked down the other side of the mountain. She had to squint to see the villages and valley far below.

She pulled her cell phone out of her pocket, pulled up her Twitter feed, and typed a quick message for her followers: "Top of the world, Ma! #summitAnnapurnaI." Then she fished her digital camera out of her rucksack. Before the climb, her publicist had asked her to pose for solo portraits when she reached the summit, but she decided to wait for Marie-Eve, Peter, and Pasang to arrive. She hadn't made it to the top on her own. She had done it as part of a team and she wanted her team to share the accomplishment.

"We did it, Doc!" Marie-Eve said when she joined her at the summit.

"Get ready to break out your ice skates," Olivia said after they shared a joyous hug.

Marie-Eve laughed. "I forgot to bring them. But I did remember this." She pulled a hockey puck out of her pocket and tossed it to Olivia. "For you, Doc. So you don't forget us when you get back to Denver."

"Not a chance." Olivia turned the puck over in her hands. Annapurna I was written on one side, Team Bradshaw on the other. The climbers' signatures were scrawled along the edges. Even Roland's, Rae's, and Sam's names appeared on the rubber disk.

Olivia ran her finger over Sam's autograph. Sam had barely acknowledged her arrival at the summit, yet she had taken part in something this thoughtful to commemorate the rest of the climb?

She glanced at Sam, standing strong and powerful as the wind buffeted her body. She seemed so at home here in this desolate, unforgiving environment. Olivia had once hoped to unravel the mystery locked in Sam's eyes. Though she knew the secret, she still didn't know the woman. Would she ever?

"Would you like me to take your picture with my camera or yours?" Sam asked.

"Use mine." Sam stepped forward and plucked the compact camera out of her hand. "It's the button on top."

Sam nodded that she understood. Olivia held the hockey puck in front of her while she, Marie-Eve, Peter, Pasang, Jimmy, and Lhakpa smiled for the camera. Jimmy wrapped a proud arm around Pasang's shoulders.

Sam took four quick shots. "Do you want to check out the pictures to make sure I didn't screw something up?"

"I'm sure they're fine, thank you."

Sam scanned the horizon. The bright blue sky was slowly being encroached by thick gray clouds. "You've got thirty more minutes before we have to descend," she said, returning the camera. "Enjoy every second."

Olivia heeded her advice. Instead of planning what was to come next, she took time to enjoy what was happening right now. She reflected on what it took to arrive at this moment and the people who had helped to get her here.

She stood with Sam, Jimmy, Lhakpa, Marie-Eve, Peter, and Pasang and enjoyed the present. The future could wait.

Sam watched Olivia's team begin to head down the mountain, taking their first steps back to the lives they had left behind. Another successful climb was almost in the books. All she needed to do now was get everyone back to BC and on the chopper to Kathmandu.

YOLANDA WALLACE

Then she could light up a celebratory cigar and enjoy some down time before she began to prepare for the next trip when she'd man the radio in BC and Rae would act as guide. This trip had had its ups and downs, but at least they were able to finish on a high. Half of the team had made it to the summit and everyone had made it out alive. She couldn't ask for more.

She allowed Lhakpa the honor of leading the descent. He was a hard worker who did his job well and without complaint. He had earned his moment in the sun. She took his place at the rear of the pack. The position was an unusual one for her, but a trip this trying needed to be viewed from a different perspective before she could pass final judgment.

After they had descended a few hundred feet, clear of the summit but still well inside the death zone, her lungs began to burn and her legs felt leaden. She was physically and mentally whipped, but this didn't feel right.

She felt like she wasn't getting enough air. She checked the gauge on her oxygen canister. According to the reading, she had enough for two more hours. Plenty of time before she needed to reach for a fresh cylinder.

But if the gauge was accurate, why was her head spinning as if the canister had already run dry?

Peter, the closest climber, was nearly fifty feet in front of her and the gap was widening with each laborious step. She needed to change canisters before she lost contact with the rest of the group, but her motor functions were already so impaired she didn't know if she could manage the feat on her own.

She fumbled for her walkie-talkie and, with a concerted effort, keyed the microphone. Her head swam. Spots swirled on the edges of her vision. She closed her eyes to combat a sudden wave of dizziness.

"Jimmy," she gasped as her heart pounded in her chest. "I need—"

The walkie-talkie fell from her hands and the ground rose to meet her. Then everything went black.

Chapter Fifteen

When Sam opened her eyes, she was lying on the most beautiful beach she had ever seen. Glossy black sand the color of onyx led to crystal clear water. Stately palm trees swayed in the gentle breeze. Overhead, the cloudless sky was a shade of blue seen only in travel magazines or upscale jewelry stores.

She stood and dusted herself off. Her feet were bare. Her cold weather gear was gone, replaced by a loose-fitting white camp shirt and a matching pair of linen pants rolled up to her calves.

She knew what she was seeing wasn't real—it was nothing more than an hallucination brought on by altitude and a lack of oxygen—but she could hear the waves crashing against the shore. Feel the warmth of the sun's rays on her skin.

She knelt and dug her fingers into the sand, grounding herself in the gritty soil. The beach was a perfect replica of one she and Bailey had visited when they had spent their first anniversary in Hawaii. They had vowed to return for their fifth anniversary but hadn't been given the chance. Mont Blanc had robbed them of the dream.

She turned in a slow circle. The beach was deserted save for herself and one lone figure that slowly approached from the north. The figure was female, tall and lithe with cornflower blond hair that fell past her shoulders. The newcomer walked as if she were keeping time with music only she could hear. Sam would recognize that walk anywhere. She used to tease its owner about it endlessly.

"Bailey."

Bailey was as beautiful as she remembered. She was wearing a pair of bright yellow flip-flops, denim cutoffs, and her favorite T-shirt. The red one with Life is Sweet emblazoned on the front. She raised a hand in greeting. "Long time no see," she said with a grin before kicking off her shoes and breaking into a run.

Sam sprinted toward her and swept her into her arms. Twelve years had passed since they had been together this way. Twelve long years that had felt like an eternity. Sam had spent countless hours longing for one last kiss. One last hug. Mercifully, she had been granted a second chance. A last chance to say good-bye.

"I never thought I'd be able to hold you like this again," she said, fighting back tears. "I've missed you so much."

Bailey caressed her face as if she were committing every feature to memory. "I've missed you, too."

They hugged again, squeezing the breath out of each other's bodies. When they broke free, Sam looked around at the tropical paradise in which they found themselves. "Is this heaven?"

"Your idea of it, yes." Bailey's expression turned serious. "But you shouldn't be here. It isn't your time."

"Then why am I here?"

"I think you know the answer as well as I do. You came to do what you couldn't do when you went back to Mont Blanc. You came to say good-bye." Bailey held Sam's hands in hers. "You've met someone, haven't you?"

Sam immediately thought of Olivia. The woman whose recklessness went in the face of her desire for caution and whose beauty made her weak in the knees. "How did you know?"

"One of the perks of being in my position," Bailey said with a familiar self-effacing grin. "You're starting to care about her, but you're afraid admitting you're developing feelings for her would mean denying your love for me. Nothing could be further from the truth. I know you love me, Sam. I feel it every day."

Sam felt an unwanted recurrence of the guilt that often threatened to overwhelm her. "I'm so sorry about what happened. If I could turn back the clock, I would do it in a heartbeat."

Bailey touched her fingers to Sam's lips. "None of that. I don't blame you for what happened. You shouldn't blame yourself. Mont Blanc is over. Don't let one day define our lives."

Sam was reminded of something Olivia had said the night she had told her about Mont Blanc. *We are who we are because of who we've lost and the way we've lost them.*

Bailey shook her shoulders as if she were shrugging off unpleasant thoughts. "We don't have much time. Let's not waste it dwelling on things we can't change."

"The past is the past. You always said that."

"Because it's true. The past should be a learning tool not a hindrance. Stop letting it hold you back, Sam. I'll always be there for you even if I can't be with you."

Bailey placed her hand on Sam's chest. Sam felt the pressure. How could a figment of her imagination feel so real?

"You have the biggest heart of anyone I've ever met. You carry enough love inside you to wrap your arms around the whole world. Don't keep that love locked away. Let it out." Bailey placed her hand under Sam's chin and tilted her face upward. "I know the real reason you're here. You came to seek my approval to move on with your life." She smiled reassuringly. "You've had my approval ever since the day we met. You don't need to ask my permission to love again. You need to give it to yourself."

Bailey's image shimmered and began to fade. The wind began to howl. Sand stung Sam's legs, arms, and face. She squinted to keep the fine particles of volcanic lava from getting in her eyes.

"What's happening?"

"Our time is up."

Sam shivered as the temperature began to drop. She could see her breath. The black sand began to turn into pristine white snow. The palm trees metamorphosed into mountains.

"It's time, Sam," Bailey said as snow began to fall. "You have to go."

Bailey began to fade even more. Her body was almost transparent now. Sam could see through her to the jagged peaks that were rising in the distance.

"Don't forget what I said." Bailey's voice was nearly lost in the roar of the wind. Sam strained to hear her. "You don't need my permission. You need yours."

Then, just like that, Bailey disappeared and Sam found herself alone.

The dream world her mind had created began to fall apart. She could hear someone's voice calling her name, but she didn't respond. The voice grew louder, more strident, then gradually began to fade away. Uncertain whether to go or stay, Sam lingered between two worlds—the real one and one of her own creation.

One of her favorite expressions was "Home is where the heart is." She lay on the snow-covered ground and let her heart decide where it wanted to call home.

CHAPTER SIXTEEN

S am's lips were blue. Her resps were so shallow Olivia could barely see the rise and fall of her chest. Her pupils were the size of pinpoints.

"Come on, Sam. Come back to me."

She gently slapped Sam's cheeks with her gloved hand. Sam's head rocked from side to side but she didn't respond. Her eyes remained closed, her features pallid and deathly still. The oxygen in the fresh canister was flowing freely—Olivia had briefly held the mask over her own face to verify there weren't any issues—but Sam wasn't coming around.

Olivia sat back on her haunches. Everyone stared at her expectantly but she didn't have any answers. "I've done all I can do. The rest is up to her. Let's get her back to camp."

Marie-Eve strapped on Sam's backpack as Jimmy, Lhakpa, Pasang, and Peter picked up Sam's limp body and began to carry her down the mountain. Olivia trailed the somber procession. The champagne waiting in Camp Six would have to remain on ice. She doubted anyone would feel like celebrating until Sam opened her eyes. Maybe not even then. Regaining consciousness would be a positive sign, but it wouldn't mean Sam was completely out of the woods. She could have suffered physical or mental impairment as a result of oxygen deprivation.

No one had seen her fall. Only Jimmy had heard her attempted cry for help. Olivia hadn't known what to think when he had suddenly turned and run past her with the walkie-talkie pressed to his ear. Then she had looked back and seen Sam lying in the snow.

Sam's oxygen canister had malfunctioned and her air supply had dwindled to almost nil. By the time Jimmy reached her, the canister was completely empty. Olivia didn't have any idea how long Sam had been without supplemental oxygen before Jimmy swapped the defective canister for a good one. Her lack of response to stimuli was troubling. If she didn't come around in the oxygen richer air of Camp Six, they'd need to descend low enough for a chopper to provide medical evac.

Olivia gritted her teeth in frustration. All her years of medical training were useless to her now. Sam's will to live was the only thing that mattered.

"I hope it's as strong as she is."

Sam opened her eyes, uncertain how much time had passed. She looked around to get her bearings and tensed up when she realized she was moving. For a brief, heart-stopping moment, she thought she had been swept up in another avalanche while she was unconscious. Then reason slowly returned. She was moving not because the hard-packed snow had given way but because someone was carrying her. She shook her head to clear the cobwebs shrouding her brain.

"She's awake," she heard Jimmy say.

"Finally." Olivia's voice this time. Her face swam into Sam's vision. Her voice was muffled by her oxygen mask, but the concern radiating from her eyes came in loud and clear. "Can you hear me?"

Sam's throat was so dry it hurt to speak. "Yes," she rasped.

"Can you walk?"

"I think so. Let me try."

"Take it easy."

Jimmy, Lhakpa, Pasang, and Peter gently lowered her to the ground, where she stood on legs as shaky as a newborn colt's. She held on to Jimmy and Lhakpa until she was sure she could move under her own power. "How long was I out?" she asked, trying to buy time until she felt secure enough to attempt to descend.

"Too long," Marie-Eve said, her face red from the exertion of carrying her own pack as well as Sam's.

"What happened?" Sam asked.

Jimmy showed her what he suspected was the source of the problem.

"Remind me to ask for a refund from our supplier when we get to Kathmandu."

Jimmy laughed and clapped her on the back. "Welcome back to the land of the living."

If only he knew how right he was, she thought.

"How do you feel?" Olivia asked.

"Better than I have in years."

Physically, she had seen better days. But mentally and emotionally, she couldn't remember the last time she had felt so good. No longer burdened by the yoke of the past, she felt as free as the phoenix tattooed on her back. She was ready to face what the future had in store. And from where she was standing, the future looked awfully bright.

The climb was almost complete, but this moment felt like a beginning not an ending. Not only did she have her life back, she had a chance to start over. She felt so giddy she almost laughed out loud.

Olivia looked at her quizzically. "What's so funny?"

"A few days ago, I was marveling at what a wonderful rapport you seemed to have with your patients. I never dreamed I was about to become one of them."

"Not for long. I'll be turning you over to Dr. Curtis as soon as we return to BC. He wants to check you out before you head down the mountain."

Sam laughed. "If the mountain didn't kill me, the truck ride might."

Jimmy pretended to take offense. "Are you making fun of my driving?"

"The truck might have four-wheel drive, but that doesn't make it an off-road vehicle, my friend."

The group laughed and joked easily as they slowly made their way down to Camp Six. Sam drew Olivia aside after they arrived.

"Do you have a minute?"

"Sure."

Sam led her away from the revelers in camp to a somewhat quieter locale. Olivia braced herself against the side of the mountain. Sam stood with her back to the wind, bearing the brunt of Mother Nature's onslaught.

"I can't possibly repay you for what you did for me up there, but I'd like to try. Can I buy you dinner as down payment? If you like Indian food, I live a floor above the best restaurant of its kind in Kathmandu. The Tandoori chicken is out of this world and the rice pudding is so good it will make you want to slap your mother. What do you say?"

She forced herself to stop talking and anxiously waited for Olivia's reply. She hadn't been this nervous asking someone for a date since she was a sixteen-year-old baby dyke who had finally realized her crushes on girls weren't just a developmental phase.

Her heart raced when she saw a flicker of interest in Olivia's eyes. The same flicker she'd seen the night before the climb began. When she had been too haunted by the past to accept what the present had to offer. But now she was ready. She was finally ready to live again. And, perhaps, to love.

But Olivia's eyes clouded over and she quickly turned away.

"Dinner sounds wonderful," she said, even though she seemed to be searching for a way to let Sam down easy, "but I'm afraid I don't have the time."

Unwilling to take no for an answer, Sam tried a different tack. "If you're in a hurry, we can settle for a couple of beers on your way to the airport."

Olivia held up her cell phone and swiped her thumb against the screen. Dozens of messages both read and unread streamed across the display. "I've been fielding interview requests almost from the moment I set foot on the summit. I'm going to be tied up from the second the chopper lands until my plane leaves on Monday. I'll barely be able to breathe let alone eat, drink, or sleep. Maybe next time?"

"Sure," Sam said disconsolately. "Next time."

But in her heart, she doubted next time would ever come.

CHAPTER SEVENTEEN

The descent went much faster than Olivia had anticipated. The group arrived in BC nearly an hour early—and with not a minute to spare.

"Can you get the chopper here any faster?" she asked Rae as the first snowflakes began to fall.

"I called them after Sam's transmission from Camp Two," Rae said. "They're already on their way. In fact, they should probably be here any minute."

"Perfect."

Olivia checked the sky. The helicopter charter company Sam and Rae relied on employed experienced pilots who were comfortable flying in all sorts of weather conditions. If the wind picked up much more, though, even those top guns would be hard-pressed to make the eighty-eight mile journey to Nepal's capital.

"How long of a drive is it?"

Rae considered the question. "The roads are winding and most of them are unpaved. The drive normally takes anywhere from five to seven hours to complete. The chopper will arrive in a fraction of that time, though turbulence will probably make the flight just as bumpy. Whether by land or by air, I think everyone will be reaching for the motion sickness pills today." To illustrate her point, she opened a bottle of Dramamine and dry-swallowed two pills. Then she slipped the slim, round container into her pocket. "I hope the flight crew packed enough barf bags."

"So do I."

Everyone gathered around the designated landing zone, where Sam addressed them for the last time. Their backpacks and assorted belongings lay at their feet.

"In all the years Rae and I have been in business, I've never been more proud of a group than I am of this one. This climb was a challenge from start to finish. It was trying. It was difficult. But it was also a pleasure. One of the most rewarding expeditions I've ever had the honor of being a part of. I was able to watch you grow. I was able to watch you become a team. And I am honored to be the person who was able to lead you to the summit." She met each person's eye, acknowledging their individual contributions one by one. She saved Olivia for last. "All the credit goes to you. Thank you for making this trip such a success."

"Hear, hear!" Peter called out, prompting a round of cheers.

"I'm not going to make the chopper ride with you," Sam said, a hint of what sounded like sadness in her voice. "I figure you've seen enough of me the past few weeks to last a lifetime, but I'm leaving you in excellent hands. Rae will take over from here. Thanks again for choosing The View from the Top."

Marie-Eve led the cheers as Sam stepped aside and let Rae take center stage.

"We shall be flying in a military-issue helicopter. That's your clue not to expect a great deal of creature comforts. We'll be flying safely, but we won't be flying in style." Safety goggles protected Rae's eyes, but her face was exposed to the elements. She turned away as the descending helicopter kicked up snow, dirt, and debris that pinged off her helmet's durable but lightweight polycarbonate shell. "Bundle up and strap yourselves in," she said after the chopper landed. "We'll be in Kat before you know it."

The group formed an orderly line and began to file inside the Russian-made helicopter. Olivia claimed a seat and looked out one of the porthole windows. Sam, Jimmy, Lhakpa, and Pasang were breaking down the remaining tents in BC and loading the heavy canvas shelters. When they were done, Lhakpa and Pasang climbed into the back of the truck, squeezing between neatly stacked piles of furniture, supplies, and equipment.

Sam and Jimmy stood at the rear of the truck, inspecting the load. Then they secured the lift gate and prepared to depart. Before she climbed into the passenger's seat, Sam turned and met Olivia's eye. Olivia gave a tentative wave as the chopper began to rise into the air. Sam doffed her cap and held it aloft like a baseball player saluting the crowd. She remained that way until the chopper banked sharply and Olivia lost sight of her.

Olivia turned away from the window feeling at odds with her warring emotions. Why did she feel such disappointment when, just a day ago, she was literally on top of the world? When she got to Kathmandu, she would finally receive the notoriety and attention she had sought at the outset of the trip. Now that both were in reach, she realized neither were what she truly wanted. What she wanted was Sam. To sit with her on a sal stump talking about whatever came to mind or, better yet, to lay with her in comfortable silence under a canopy of stars not saying anything at all.

As expected, Annapurna I had given her the adventure of a lifetime. She had met every challenge the mountain had thrown at her, but in her rush to reach the summit and establish her legacy, she had failed to meet the one challenge that mattered most.

Instead of challenging herself to explore her feelings for Sam, she had chosen to ignore them. By doing so, she had denied herself a chance at something that meant more than anything she had ever accomplished.

She had turned down a chance at love.

People waited all their lives for a chance at something this good. She couldn't let hers pass her by.

CHAPTER EIGHTEEN

Sam maneuvered her scooter through traffic. On Kathmandu's narrow, congested streets, a car was often more of a hindrance than a convenience. Her scooter allowed her to squeeze through most traffic snarls and avoid time-consuming delays. When she couldn't find clear stretches of road, she detoured over sidewalks or down back alleys.

She lived on New Road. The thoroughfare was the busiest in Nepal. Restaurants and shops lined both sides of the street. Vehicles of all varieties clogged all four lanes. She made it home from the warehouse on the edge of town in a little over sixty minutes. Not bad for rush hour.

She climbed off her scooter with a sense of relief. The climb was over, the truck and the supplies were in storage, and her clients had scattered. Now it was time to relax. She locked her scooter in the rack in front of her building and stepped onto the sidewalk.

She lived above Naan, the bustling restaurant where she had hoped to treat Olivia to dinner. Through the restaurant's wide front window, she could see platters of food being taken to eager patrons. The fragrant smells of rogan josh and pork vindaloo made her mouth water, but the siren call of a hot shower was too powerful to ignore. She placed a to-go order, paid in advance, and instructed the courier to leave the food outside her door if she didn't respond to his knock.

A narrow stairway to the left of the restaurant's entrance led to an apartment two floors above. Her place.

She climbed the stairs and unlocked the door. Closing the door behind her, she dropped her backpack in the foyer and hung her coat on the rack. The walls were painted a relaxing sky blue. A navy blue plaid couch and a matching armchair were positioned in front of a tiny television set not much bigger than a microwave. She kept meaning to buy a bigger set, but she wasn't home often enough to enjoy it so she didn't see the point. She tossed her keys on the sturdy teak coffee table and took off her boots.

The small living room led to a cramped but neatly organized galley kitchen. A double sink and laminate-topped counter were on one side of the kitchen, a refrigerator and gas stove on the other. Glass-front cabinets lined both walls. Copper-bottomed pots and pans hung on a graffiti-covered pegboard, providing an imaginative bent to what could have been a humdrum display. The pegboard had been Pasang's idea, but she had come to love it as much as he had when he'd helped pick it out and asked some of his friends to decorate it for her.

Her dining area consisted of a curvy wrought iron bistro table and two café-style chairs of similar design. She thought the setup would have looked right at home on a Paris street. The only things missing were a view of the Eiffel Tower and the sound of accordion music playing in the background.

Sam paused to straighten the framed photo of her favorite fishing hole hanging above the couch, then headed to the bathroom. She undressed on the way, leaving discarded articles of clothing in her wake.

She stepped in the shower and turned on the spray. She sighed in satisfaction as hot water cascaded over her body, loosening the knots and soothing her assorted aches.

"God, it's good to be home."

Several long minutes later, she rinsed shampoo out of her hair, turned off the water, and reached for a towel. She slowly dried off and stepped out of the shower. Her hair, so thick it took forever to air dry, dripped water down her bare back as she stood naked on the cold tile floor.

She put on some sweats and a long-sleeved T-shirt and peeked outside her door, where her food was waiting. She set the main course on the kitchen counter, placed dessert in the refrigerator, and returned to the living room, where she lit a cigar and sorted through the mail that had accumulated while she was away. She was almost done when someone knocked on her door. She clenched her cigar between her teeth and padded barefoot to the door. The neighborhood kids loved hearing about her climbs, but they usually gave her a day or two to recover before they pestered her for stories.

"You guys are starting early this time, aren't you?" she asked in Nepali.

She opened the door expecting to be besieged by a sea of eager faces. Instead, she was confronted by only one.

Olivia stood in the doorway, a six-pack tucked under her arm. "How about that beer?" she asked cheerily. "Gorkha's your brand, isn't it?"

For a second, Sam thought she was hallucinating again. But the woman standing in her doorway—and on the threshold of her heart—was no dream. More like a dream come true.

"If you don't have any Schell's, Gorkha will do."

Olivia grinned. "I'll be sure to pick up some Schell's the next time I'm in Minnesota. In the meantime, may I come in?"

"Of course." With a start, Sam realized she was still blocking Olivia's way. She moved to one side and ushered Olivia into her apartment. "May I take your coat?" she asked, finding her manners.

"Yes, please."

Olivia shrugged off her parka and Sam hung it on the rack. She extinguished her cigar and put the six-pack in the refrigerator while Olivia looked around her apartment.

"I thought you had interviews lined up," she said, popping the caps on two of the bottles.

"Change of plans," Olivia said after Sam returned to the living room. She accepted the proffered beer and sat on the couch. "Or, more accurately, a change in priorities."

"Yeah?" Wary of being rejected again, Sam tried not to read too much into Olivia's unexpected appearance on her doorstep. "How did that work out for you?"

Olivia took a sip of her beer and nodded appreciatively. "I asked myself what was most important to me. Lo and behold, you came out on top."

Sam's heart skittered in her chest. "Call me stupid, but I need you to spell it out for me." She draped her arm across the back of the couch. "What exactly are you trying to say?"

"I'm saying yes."

"To?"

Olivia set her bottle of beer on the coffee table and rested her hand on Sam's arm. "Every question you've ever asked me. Every question you will ever ask me."

"*Every* question? That could be dangerous."

"I don't care. When the chopper took off today, I realized I didn't come to Nepal to climb Annapurna I. I came here to meet you. Now that I have, I don't ever want to leave you."

Olivia cupped Sam's cheek in her palm. Sam felt grounded by her touch, even as Olivia's words made her soul take flight.

Sam leaned forward until her lips met Olivia's in a kiss so tender it brought tears to her eyes.

"I hope you don't mind if I put you to the test," she said.

"How so?"

Sam's omnipresent Twins cap was surprisingly absent, revealing a thick shock of short salt-and-pepper hair. Olivia ran her hands through the unruly tresses.

"I want to know if you really will say yes to everything."

Olivia smiled as Sam turned her toward her and placed one of her legs on either side of her body.

"There are limits to everything, you know."

"I know."

She felt herself grow hard as Sam scooted her closer and cupped her ass in the palms of her hands. She wrapped her arms around Sam's neck as Sam drew her into her lap.

"What's your first question?"

"Do you want to be with me?"

"Yes."

Olivia tried not to gasp when Sam's hands worked their way inside her many layers of clothes and slid against her bare skin.

"Are you sure?"

Sam tilted her face toward hers. Olivia drew Sam's breath into her mouth then claimed her lips in a kiss.

"Yes."

Sam's full lips curled into a smile. "Are you hungry?"

Olivia slipped her hands under Sam's T-shirt and cradled her firm breasts in her hands. "Yes."

Sam moaned and her hips rose to meet Olivia's. "Do you like Indian food?"

"Yes." Olivia brushed her thumbs over Sam's nipples until the sensitive flesh turned rock hard. Sam's blue eyes turned almost black.

"I've got some food in the kitchen, but it might not be enough for two. Would you like to see a menu?"

"Yes."

Olivia raised her arms as Sam pulled her Henley over her head. Her silk undershirt quickly followed. Then Sam's long-sleeved T-shirt joined the growing pile.

Sam lay back on the couch and slowly ran her hands up Olivia's windsuit-covered thighs. Olivia hooked her thumbs in the waistband of Sam's sweats and slowly slid them over the curve of her ass.

"Now I have some questions for you," Olivia said as her fingers explored the patch of dark hair at the apex of Sam's thighs. "The restaurant downstairs. Is it where you were planning to take me for dinner?" Sam squirmed beneath her, making her feel like a cowboy riding a bucking bronco.

"Yes."

Olivia brushed her lips against the side of Sam's neck. She skimmed Sam's cheek and came to a stop next to her ear. She caressed the lobe with her tongue and slowly drew it into her mouth. She was rewarded with a hiss of pleasure. "And I assume they do takeout?"

"Yes." Sam nodded fervently. "There's a menu in the kitchen. I already know what I want. How about you?"

"Yes."

"So dinner can wait?"

Olivia smiled down at her. "Yes."

Smiling, Sam sat up and slowly traced the outline of Olivia's mouth with her tongue. Olivia groaned deep in her throat and pressed her body's full length against Sam's. Sam opened her mouth and allowed Olivia's probing tongue inside. Olivia's tongue danced against hers, tentatively at first then with purpose.

Olivia slipped a hand between their bodies and cupped Sam's breast. She teased the hardened nipple with her thumb. Sam kneaded Olivia's hip. She placed her leg between Olivia's. Olivia rode her thigh, the muscles in her hips flexing against Sam's hand.

"If that's the appetizer," she said when her rapid breathing finally slowed, "I can't imagine how good the main course is going to be."

Sam twined her fingers through Olivia's hair. "Wait until you see dessert. Follow me."

Sam grabbed a container out of the refrigerator, took Olivia's hand, and led her to the bedroom. Olivia had to talk herself out of turning the trip into a race. Continuing to follow Sam's lead, she sat cross-legged on the bed. Sam sat in front of her. Sam opened the small container in her hands. Olivia peered inside. The dish smelled sweet yet spicy. Rice, coconut milk, and sugar infused with cardamom. Slivered almonds and golden raisins were sprinkled on top.

"Kheer is a dish vital to Indian culture," Sam said. "No ceremony, feast, or celebration is complete without it. In some parts of the country, tradition says a wedding isn't fully blessed unless kheer is served at the reception."

She dipped her fingers into the rice pudding and held them out. Olivia slowly licked her fingers clean. "Are you asking me to marry you?"

Sam offered her another serving. "One step at a time," she said with an inscrutable smile.

Olivia licked her lips. "What's step one?"

Sam took some kheer for herself. "We're taking it right now." She placed the container on the nightstand and moved to step two.

She unhooked Olivia's bra and slid it down her arms. Then she kissed Olivia's shoulders and worked her way down to Olivia's breasts. Olivia arched her back when Sam's mouth closed around her nipple. Sam flicked it with the tip of her tongue. Rolled it between her teeth. Then she moved to Olivia's other breast and gave it the same treatment.

Moaning, Olivia lay back on the bed and pulled Sam down on top of her.

As her hands and mouth continued to touch and tease, Sam grabbed the waistband of Olivia's pants and pushed them past her knees, then tugged them off. She reached inside Olivia's gray boy shorts. Her fingers raked through the tight curls.

Olivia panted in anticipation. The touch she had been expecting took her breath away. Sam's finger stroked the length of her clit and circled the tip. Olivia gasped when Sam dipped a finger inside—and whined when she quickly withdrew.

Sam pulled off Olivia's underwear and tossed them over her shoulder. Her eyes slowly traveled up Olivia's body.

Olivia lay naked on the bed, her body and soul exposed for Sam's thorough inspection.

"You're amazing," Sam whispered.

"Not half as much as you are."

Sam trailed her fingers up the inside of Olivia's calves. When she reached Olivia's knees, she replaced her fingers of her right hand with her tongue.

The muscles in Olivia's thighs quivered. Her legs parted almost of their own accord. Sam's mouth closed around her center. Sam's tongue teased her clit.

"Ah, fuck." She pressed her head against the pillow as her hips rose to meet Sam's mouth.

Sam quickly brought her to the brink. Olivia gritted her teeth to hold the end at bay. She didn't want her first time with Sam to come to an end so soon. But the need for Sam to take her—to claim her—was just too strong.

"I need you inside me."

Sam slipped one finger inside her before adding another. Her legs held Olivia's apart. The rough fabric of the bedspread contrasted with the softness of her touch. She kissed Olivia, her tongue filling her mouth.

Olivia moved against Sam's fingers. White heat formed in her center and spread throughout her body. "Yes," she hissed. "Right there."

Sam kissed her hungrily. As if she wanted to taste her pleasure. Olivia made sure she got her fill. Sam's thumb massaged her clit while her fingers plumbed her depths. Olivia dug her heels into the mattress.

"God, Sam."

She screamed in release as her body came apart.

Sam waited for her to come down, then gently withdrew her fingers. "Are you okay?" She stroked Olivia's hair. "Did I hurt you?" Her voice was filled with so much tenderness the sound melted Olivia's heart.

"You were perfect. You made me feel like there was no one else in the world. Like no one else mattered. Now it's my turn to return the favor."

Olivia slid her nails over the contours of Sam's rippled stomach. Sam shuddered against her, then raised herself to her knees.

Olivia sat up in bed. She ran her hands over Sam's strong shoulders and down her chest. She cupped Sam's firm breasts in her hands. Sam's nipples were light brown and rock hard. Olivia reverently kissed one then the other.

Moving lower, she circled Sam's navel with her tongue and nipped at the skin. She could smell the sweet scent of Sam's arousal.

Sam bent to kiss her. Her tongue was insistent, betraying her need. Olivia positioned her face down on the bed. Sam tried to roll over on her back, but Olivia held her in place.

"It's okay. I'm not going to hurt you."

She wanted Sam to trust her, but trust couldn't be asked for. It had to be earned. The next few minutes would tell if she had proven herself worthy of Sam's trust.

Moving slowly and deliberately, she placed one knee on either side of Sam's hips. Before her, the dramatic tattoo on Sam's back was displayed in all its glory.

Olivia sank her fingers into the dimples of Venus, the symmetrical indentations in Sam's lower back. She touched the tattoo, passing through the leaping flames, over the brightly colored tail and taloned feet, up the feathered body, and past the open mouth. When she came to the outstretched wings, she lowered her body, dragged her nipples across Sam's back, and arched away.

Sam sucked in her breath, caught between wanting to give pleasure and receive it. Olivia's tongue traveled up her spine, moving from the cleft of her hips to the nape of her neck. Then Olivia blew on the thin trail of moisture she'd left behind. The warm tongue followed by the cool air fanned the flames of Sam's arousal. If Olivia was trying to make her feel like there was no one else in the world, she was doing a damn fine job of it. Olivia made her feel sexy. Desirable. Moreover, she made her feel loved.

Her eyes filled with tears. Olivia must have seen them. She kissed her cheek and smoothed her hair.

"Okay?"

Sam nodded. Olivia rolled her over. She kissed her as if she meant to steady her nerves, but Sam's nerves were gone. Any doubts she might have been harboring disappeared as soon as Olivia covered her body with her own. Sam wanted this. She wanted Olivia. Tonight. Tomorrow. Every day for the rest of their lives.

Olivia moved lower. She parted Sam with her tongue. Sam was so wet she was surprised Olivia didn't drown. She squeezed her eyelids shut but quickly opened them again. When she came, she wanted to be gazing into the eyes of the woman she loved. The woman she loved. The words no longer frightened her. Could no longer be denied.

When Bailey died, she'd thought she would never find love again. She'd thought she would never be able to let anyone else into her heart. Almost without her being aware of it, Olivia had taken up residence there. When had she moved in? She had knocked on the door the day they met. Then she'd spent the next six weeks leaving pieces of herself behind.

Sam knew Olivia's heart. She knew her soul. Now she knew her body as well. Sam had provided most of the same introductions. Now it was time to make the final one.

She offered herself to Olivia. Opened herself fully and completely. She looked down at Olivia. With her eyes, she asked an unspoken question. *Will you take me as I am?* Olivia's tongue provided an unequivocal yes.

When it was over, Sam held Olivia in her arms. She said the words she never thought she'd say again.

"I love you."

Olivia lifted her head. Her smile was a beacon leading Sam out of her self-imposed darkness once and for all. "I love you, too."

EPILOGUE

Olivia followed Sam up the trail, a beautiful but rugged stretch of earth in Yellowknife, the capital of Canada's Northwest Territories. They had been hiking for hours, but Sam promised the view from the top would be worth the effort.

"Are you going to be able to make it to Pasang's wedding?" Olivia asked. The temperature was in the mid-forties, almost cold enough for her to be able to see her breath.

Sam looked back at her and grinned. "Jimmy would kill me—kill *us*—if we missed it. Pasang and Peter would, too." Sam laughed. "There's no telling what Rae and Marie-Eve might do."

"I don't think we want to find out."

Though she maintained a heavy work schedule, Rae was a constant fixture at Marie-Eve's hockey games and often flew in to visit Olivia and Sam in their home in Colorado. She conveniently went missing, however, whenever the time came to babysit Chance and Gigi's infant twins. Olivia and Sam, on the other hand, were never able to say no. Beatriz and C.J. had both of them wrapped around their chubby little fingers.

"Nothing's going to stop me from watching the boys get hitched," Sam said. "After I finish the expedition to Mt. Fuji, I'll swing by Everest."

"I'll meet you there."

"Don't forget to bring my tux."

"As long as you don't forget to pick up the Gorkha."

For the past year, they had shared a home and a life. Both had drastically reduced their schedules but hadn't been able to eliminate all of their commitments. Whenever possible, they synchronized their calendars to limit their time apart. Each reunion was like meeting for the first time. Olivia looked forward to going to work, but she looked forward to coming home even more. Because now she had someone to come home to.

The trip to Everest for Pasang and Peter's wedding would be Sam's second trip to Nepal this year and Olivia's first since Annapurna I. Olivia couldn't wait to return to the country where she had met the love of her life. But first things first.

"Here we are," Sam said when they reached the summit.

She spread a thick wool blanket on the lush grass and placed a picnic basket on one corner to weight it down. Kneeling on the blanket, she offered Olivia her hand.

Olivia lay on her back and stared up at the night sky. Sam lay next to her. A rainbow of light danced overhead. Colorful bands of red, yellow, blue, and green outshone the manmade lights twinkling faintly in the valley below.

"Welcome to our own private light show," Sam said.

Olivia indicated the group of tourists slowly making their way up an adjacent ridge. "Not so private."

Sam pulled a thermos out of the picnic basket, unscrewed the top, and poured two cups of hot chocolate. "I can't give you the world, babe. I can only show it to you one mountain at a time."

"One down and how many to go?"

Sam laughed, once a rarity but now a common occurrence. "I hope you packed your traveling shoes, Doc. This could take a while."

Olivia took a sip of her hot chocolate. "Fine by me. I've got nothing but time."

About the Author

Yolanda Wallace is not a professional writer, but she plays one in her spare time. She has written four previous novels, *In Medias Res*, *Rum Spring*, *Lucky Loser*, and *Month of Sundays*. *Her* short stories have appeared in multiple anthologies including *Romantic Interludes 2: Secrets* and *Women of the Dark Streets*. She and her partner live in beautiful coastal Georgia—about as far from the mountains of Nepal as you can get. They are parents to four children of the four-legged variety—a boxer and three cats. Yolanda can be reached at yolandawrites@gmail.com.

Books Available from Bold Strokes Books

Sea Glass Inn by Karis Walsh. When Melinda Andrews commissions a series of mosaics by Pamela Whitford for her new inn, she doesn't expect to be more captivated by the artist than by the paintings. (978-1-60282-771-4)

The Awakening: A Sisterhood of Spirits Novel by Yvonne Heidt. Sunny Skye has interacted with spirits her entire life but when she runs into Officer Jordan Lawson during a ghost investigation, she discovers more than just facts in a missing girl's cold case file. (978-1-60282-772-1)

Murphy's Law by Yolanda Wallace. No matter how high you climb, you can't escape your past. (978-1-60282-773-8)

Blacker Than Blue by Rebekah Weatherspoon. Threatened with losing her first love to a powerful demon, vampire Cleo Jones is willing to break the ultimate law of the undead to rebuild the family she has lost. (978-1-60282-774-5)

Another 365 Days by KE Payne. Clemmie Atkins is back, and her life is more complicated than ever before! Still madly in love with her girlfriend, Clemmie suddenly finds her life turned upside down with distractions, confessions, and the return of a familiar face. (978-1-60282-775-2)

Tricks of the Trade: Magical Gay Erotica edited by Jerry L. Wheeler. Today's hottest erotica writers take you inside the sultry, seductive world of magicians and their tricks—professional and otherwise. (978-1-60282-781-3)

Straight Boy Roommate by Kev Troughton. Tom isn't expecting much from his first term at University, but a chance encounter with straight boy Dan catapults him into an extraordinary, wild weekend of sex and self-discovery, which turns his life upside down, and leads him into his first love affair. (978-1-60282-782-0)

Silver Collar by Gill McKnight. Werewolf Luc Garoul is outlawed and out of control, but can her family track her down before a sinister predator gets there first? Fourth in the Garoul series. (978-1-60282-764-6)

The Dragon Tree Legacy by Ali Vali. For Aubrey Tarver time hasn't dulled the pain of losing her first love Wiley Gremillion, but she has to set that aside when her choices put her life and her family's lives in real danger. (978-1-60282-765-3)

The Midnight Room by Ronica Black. After a chance encounter with the mysterious and brooding Lillian Gray in the "midnight room" of The Griffin, a local lesbian bar, confident and gorgeous Audrey McCarthy learns that her bad girl behavior isn't bulletproof. (978-1-60282-766-0)

Dirty Sex by Ashley Bartlett. Vivian Cooper and twins Reese and Ryan DiGiovanni stole a lot of money and the guy they took it from wants it back. Like now. (978-1-60282-767-7)

Raising Hell: Demonic Gay Erotica edited by Todd Gregory. *Raising Hell*: hot stories of gay erotica featuring demons. (978-1-60282-768-4)

Pursued by Joel Gomez-Dossi. Openly gay college student Jamie Bradford becomes romantically involved with two men at the same time, and his hell begins when one of his boyfriends becomes intent on killing him. (978-1-60282-769-1)

The Storm by Shelley Thrasher. Rural East Texas. 1918. War-weary Jaq Bergeron and marriage-scarred musician Molly Russell try to salvage love from the devastation of the war abroad and natural disasters at home. (978-1-60282-780-6)

Crossroads by Radclyffe. Dr. Hollis Monroe specializes in short-term relationships but when she meets pregnant mother-to-be Annie

Colfax, fate brings them together at a crossroads that will change their lives forever. (978-1-60282-756-1)

Beyond Innocence by Carsen Taite. When a life is on the line, love has to wait. Doesn't it? (978-1-60282-757-8)

Heart Block by Melissa Brayden. Socialite Emory Owen and struggling single mom Sarah Matamoros are perfectly suited for each other but face a difficult time when trying to merge their contrasting worlds and the people in them. If love truly exists, can it find a way? (978-1-60282-758-5)

Pride and Joy by M.L. Rice. Perfect Bryce Montgomery is her parents' pride and joy, but when they discover that their daughter is a lesbian, her world changes forever. (978-1-60282-759-2)

Timothy by Greg Herren. Timothy is a romantic suspense thriller from award-winning mystery writer Greg Herren set in the fabulous Hamptons. (978-1-60282-760-8)

In Stone: A Grotesque Faerie Tale by Jeremy Jordan King. A young New Yorker is rescued from a hate crime by a mysterious someone who turns out to be more of a *something*. (978-1-60282-761-5)

The Jesus Injection by Eric Andrews-Katz. Murderous statues, demented drag queens, political bombings, ex-gay ministries, espionage, and romance are all in a day's work for a top-secret agent. But the gloves are off when Agent Buck 98 comes up against The Jesus Injection. (978-1-60282-762-2)

Combustion by Daniel W. Kelly. Bearish detective Deck Waxer comes to the city of Kremfort Cove to investigate why the hottest men in town are bursting into flames in broad daylight. (978-1-60282-763-9)

Ladyfish by Andrea Bramhall. Finn's escape to the Florida Keys leads her straight into the arms of scuba diving instructor Oz as she fights for her freedom, their blossoming love...and her life! (978-1-60282-747-9)

Spanish Heart by Rachel Spangler. While on a mission to find herself in Spain, Ren Molson runs the risk of losing her heart to her tour guide, Lina Montero. (978-1-60282-748-6)

Love Match by Ali Vali. When Parker "Kong" King, the number one tennis player in the world, meets commercial pilot Captain Sydney Parish, sparks fly—but not from attraction. They have the summer to see if they have a love match. (978-1-60282-749-3)

One Touch by L.T. Marie. A romance writer and a travel agent come together at their high school reunion, only to find out that the memory of that one touch never fades. (978-1-60282-750-9)

Night Shadows: Queer Horror edited by Greg Herren and J.M. Redmann. *Night Shadows* features delightfully wicked stories by some of the biggest names in queer publishing. (978-1-60282-751-6)

Secret Societies by William Holden. An outcast hustler, his unlikely "mother," his faithless lovers, and his religious persecutors—all in 1726. (978-1-60282-752-3)

The Raid by Lee Lynch. Before Stonewall, having a drink with friends or your girl could mean jail. Would these women and men still have family, a job, a place to live after...The Raid? (978-1-60282-753-0)

The You Know Who Girls: Freshman Year by Annameekee Hesik. As they begin freshman year, Abbey Brooks and her best friend, Kate, pinkie swear they'll keep away from the lesbians in Gila High, but Abbey already suspects she's one of those you-know-who girls herself and slowly learns who her true friends really are. (978-1-60282-754-7)

Wyatt: Doc Holliday's Account of an Intimate Friendship by Dale Chase. Erotica writer Dale Chase takes the remarkable friendship between Wyatt Earp, upright lawman, and Doc Holliday, Southern gentlemen turned gambler and killer, to an entirely new level: hot! (978-1-60282-755-4)

Month of Sundays by Yolanda Wallace. Love doesn't always happen overnight; sometimes it takes a month of Sundays. (978-1-60282-739-4)

Jacob's War by C.P. Rowlands. ATF Special Agent Allison Jacob's task force is in the middle of an all-out war, from the streets to the boardrooms of America. Small business owner Katie Blackburn is the latest victim who accidentally breaks it wide open, but she may break AJ's heart at the same time. (978-1-60282-740-0)

The Pyramid Waltz by Barbara Ann Wright. Princess Katya Nar Umbriel wants a perfect romance, but her Fiendish nature and duties to the crown mean she can never tell the truth—until she meets Starbride, a woman who gets to the heart of every secret, even if it will be the death of her. (978-1-60282-741-7)

The Secret of Othello by Sam Cameron. Florida teen detectives Steven and Denny risk their lives to search for a sunken NASA satellite—but under the waves, no one can hear you scream... (978-1-60282-742-4)

Finding Bluefield by Elan Barnehama. Set in the backdrop of Virginia and New York and spanning the years 1960–1982, *Finding Bluefield* chronicles the lives of Nicky Stewart, Barbara Philips, and their son, Paul, as they struggle to define themselves as a family. (978-1-60282-744-8)